GOD'S DIPLOMAT

GOD'S DIPLOMAT

Gordon Strachan

VANTAGE PRESS
New York

Published by Vantage Press, Inc.
516 West 34th Street, New York, New York 10001

Manufactured in the United States of America
ISBN: 0-533-09704-5

Library of Congress Catalog Card No.: 91-91046

0 9 8 7 6 5 4 3 2 1

To my wife, Ann, my daughter, Angela, my mother, Jean, and Duncan . . . without whose help this book would not have been published

GOD'S DIPLOMAT

ONE

As I woke this morning I couldn't help but wonder who had phoned earlier. That was around seven o'clock; it was now ten o'clock. I wasn't feeling too well after last night's party at the American embassy. I had gone there with Sir George Anders, who was my boss at the Foreign Office. We both had had one over the top, drinkwise, and he was holding up better than I was. Lucky for me the secretary at the embassy was also my date for the following night. Janet had called me a taxi and seen that the driver was paid. I was hoping Janet would be coming home with me, but she was on duty.

My head was pounding; I needed something to cure it. The caller this morning had asked me to meet him at twelve o'clock at the Kings Arms, which was my local. I slammed the phone down before he had finished. Between how I was feeling and what he had said, something made me think someone was pulling my leg. He had said he had something of national importance to tell me and would I meet him at the Kings Arms? Slamming the phone down seemed like a good idea at the time. It could have been Frank or John, who are two of my workmates at the Foreign Office. John was quite capable of the phone call, as I had put one over on him a few months ago.

As it was Sunday, the pub wouldn't open till twelve-thirty. That was another mistake the caller had made; my local didn't open till half an hour after the time he had mentioned. Well, I had a shaky shave and dressed. The pub had been open for half an hour, as it was one o'clock.

As I walked into the bar, Mary, the barmaid, caught my eye and shouted, "The usual, David?"

I said, "Yes, and add a small scotch, too." Though only open a half hour before I arrived, the bar was quite busy. There were about twenty people standing and sitting about. I couldn't see anyone I knew. Mary came over to where I was standing, and I asked her had anyone been asking for me. She said no.

An hour passed, so my thoughts about a leg pull had been confirmed. I finished my pint and moved toward the toilet before going home. I had just opened the first door leading to the toilet, when the second door I was about to go through blew straight into me. I just heard the explosion before I blacked out.

It was three days later that I came out of a haze in Saint Mark's Hospital. Funny enough, the first thing that entered my head was "some bloody leg pull." I would have laughed if my leg and chest had let me; they were both giving me great pain. Just then a nurse came in. She asked me how I felt.

I was just about to reply when a doctor entered. He said, "How are you, Mr. Martin?"

I told him my chest felt like it was in a vice and my leg was very painful. I couldn't seem to get my head off the pillow.

"Well, Mr. Martin, we'll give you something for the pain, but first do you think you could talk to two policemen who are waiting outside?"

I said okay. I was curious to find out what had happened at the Kings Arms.

The two policemen introduced themselves as Detective Inspector Frazer and Sergeant Morgan.

"Well, Mr. Martin, can you tell us anything you can remember about what happened at the pub?" one asked.

I replied, "Not too much, I'm afraid. After the door hit

me, I blacked out. The next thing I remember is waking up here."

He then asked if I was to meet anyone at the pub or was it just a casual visit. I didn't want to tell them about the phone call, just in case they checked with the office.

Frank and John wouldn't find it funny having two policemen turn up at the Foreign Office. I then turned to the doctor and said I wasn't feeling too good, which I wasn't. The inspector said he would call back tomorrow when I felt better. The doctor then told me I had four broken ribs and my leg was broken in two places. I also had a slight concussion, which was why I couldn't lift my head off the pillow. The nurse came in and gave me a jag, which put me to sleep in five minutes. Before I dropped off, I remembered I hadn't asked the inspector what had actually happened.

I was woken with the nurse nudging my arm; my body still felt like someone was hitting me with a cricket bat. I asked what time it was. She said 6 A.M. I forgot this was the N.H.S. and they were no slouches in getting you wakened in the mornings. She asked if I felt like eating anything. I said no, but a cup of tea would go down well. To that she replied that the doctor would be around shortly and after he left I could have tea.

It was 9 A.M. before I saw the doctor, and ten o'clock before I saw the cup of tea. The doctor said I would be kept in for two weeks before going home. Just after I had finished my tea, the nurse told me I had a visitor. It was Janet. She looked worried as she asked how I felt. I said a bit better now that she was here. She laughed at that and cheered up some. She kissed me on the cheek. I said she could do better than that. She said I looked too fragile for anything stronger. I asked her what the news of the explosion was. She said that seven people had been killed and several seriously injured. They had not got anyone in connection with the blast. She tried to change the subject by telling me that Frank and John would be seeing me later.

Frank and John turned up with Sir George. The hospital was sticking to the official visiting hours, seven till eight. Sir George was the first to speak, telling me that everybody at the office was asking for me. Sir George said he couldn't stay too long, as he was involved in the incident with the home secretary. They were looking at the possibility of it being an IRA attack, but as for why, no one could fathom it. Sir George wasn't one for handing out too much sympathy. He bid me a good-bye and hoped I would be better soon.

Frank and John hadn't said much while Sir George was speaking, but they both drew closer to the bed when he left. Frank asked how I was. I told him I was not too bad and what the doctor had said. John was smiling as if ready to tell me one of his jokes, but before he could say anything, I asked him if he had phoned me the Sunday of the explosion. He replied, "It wasn't me, old son. I had better things to do, especially with the little brunette I picked up at the party. Why do you ask?"

I told him someone had phoned my place early on Sunday morning and asked me to meet them, or should I say him, at the Kings Arms. John wanted to know what the caller was after. I told him, "I don't know, John. I thought it was you or Frank having a leg pull. I slammed down the phone before he got to that."

Frank asked if I thought the call had anything to do with the suspected IRA bomb. I told him I just didn't know. The visiting hour was nearly up, so they both said they would try to get to see me before the end of the week.

I was beginning to feel tired again. The nurse came in and said if I wanted anything to ring the buzzer beside the bed. I said, "Thank you, nurse," and was sleeping within seconds.

At first I thought I was dreaming. There was this giant of a man, standing beside the bed. He had shoulder-length hair and appeared to be wearing a robe of white. His eyes seemed to glow from his face; he was very darkly tanned. The robe looked like those worn in Arab countries.

I tried to say something, but nothing would come out. My next thought was to press the buzzer beside my bed, but my arm wouldn't move.

He moved closer to the bed and put his hand on my shoulder. His voice seemed to come from a far distance. "I am the one who called you on Sunday, the same day as the explosion. We are sorry for what happened at your place of drink. It is regrettable, but unfortunately not foreseen. We require your help in stopping your country from becoming involved in a nuclear war."

A nuclear war! What the hell was he on about. *This must be a nightmare from the effects of the explosion,* I thought. But he was still there talking.

"I will return tomorrow and wish you to come with me when I do."

He turned and went out the door.

I tried to move my arm; it seemed okay. I pressed the buzzer. The nurse was in my room in seconds. I asked her who had been in my room. She laughed and said no one had been in, as she was at her desk all the time, only a few yards from my door. She said I must have had a dream, as no one was allowed a visit at two in the morning. She then tucked me in as if I had been a naughty little boy. "Get some sleep, Mr. Martin. I'll see you in a couple of hours." At that, she left.

She half convinced me that it was a dream, but it seemed so real. My next thought was to try to get some sleep and maybe get that so-called dream back again.

I woke with the nurse pushing a trolley through the door. "Time for a bath, Mr. Martin. Any more nightmares?"

I just glared at her. She got the message.

Janet managed to talk her way in to see me for an early visit. It was only eleven o'clock. "Hi, David, how are you today? I've managed to wangle some time off from the embassy to see you."

She looked radiant. "Plant one on my lips, Janet, just to make sure I'm not dreaming. You look beautiful."

She kissed me lingeringly, then laughed. "You're getting better, alright."

I thought about telling her what happened earlier this morning, then thought better of it. She would likely think along the same lines as the nurse, that it was all a dream. She said Sir George and the lads would get in to see me whenever they could. There seemed to be some kind of crisis in the Middle East and everyone was getting involved in some manner. This made my heart pound after what had happened this morning.

"Do you know what the crisis is all about?" I asked.

She said no, only that they weren't going to intervene or mediate. What she was saying made last night seem more real than just a dream.

After Janet left, I started to turn things over in my head, but nothing was making sense. Why was I involved? If what the giant had said was true, how could I help, lying here with a broken leg and cracked ribs? I conceded it wasn't worth the strain until I knew more of what was going on.

At dinnertime the two nurses came in and pulled me up to a sitting position. It was painful, but I felt famished and thought the pain would be worth it if the dinner was okay.

The nurse had just taken the dinner tray away when he appeared. He was as big as I had thought. This time I was going to get in the first word before he did. I was just going to ask who he was, but like this morning I couldn't get anything out.

It was frightening to think it was he who had caused my voice to stop.

"I'm not going to hurt you, David; just listen to what I have to say. As I told you last night, or should I say this morning, we need your help; time is not, I'm afraid, on our side. I am going to give you your voice back. You will no doubt have many questions to ask me. I hope you will keep them to a minimum. You can speak now, David."

I coughed before speaking, just to make sure I could. "Who are you? What's your name?"

"Slow down, David, one thing at a time. My name is Peter. I am part of a group who are working together to prevent your country from nuclear war."

"But why have you picked me? I don't have that much power. I'm only a junior minister to Sir George Anders, and anyway, I couldn't move two yards. My injuries from the explosion won't allow it."

"Do you have any clothes in the room you could wear?"

I told him, "Yes, in the cupboard over there."

He moved toward the cupboard. As he put his hand in for my clothes, he told me to get up.

I was beginning to get mad at this suggestion. I had had enough of this lunatic telling me to do things any normal person knew were impossible. My anger had made me jump to a sitting position. I didn't even feel any pain.

He was looking at me with the clothes in his hand. I had swung my legs over the side of the bed and sat there stunned. As I looked at my leg, which was supposed to be in plaster, the plaster was lying on the floor. There wasn't even a mark on my leg. The strapping round my chest was loose. I no longer had any pain when I breathed, as was the case before.

I stood up and moved toward the giant. I thought I had better stop thinking in terms of him being a giant; it might come out in my speech. If he could do what he had done to me in friendship, I didn't want to get on the wrong side of him. While I dressed, Peter told me where we were going. He had another three friends who would be helping us in trying to prevent the war. They were at an address about ten miles outside London, at a farm called the Grange.

I was pretty nervous thinking someone might come in while I was dressing. I asked Peter how we were going to get by the duty nurse, who was only yards away from the door; plus we had all the corridors to navigate before we were outside. I felt great and was ready to go. Peter would stick out like a sore thumb; his garb and size made him anything but inconspicuous.

"Let's go," he said.

He opened the door. The nurse on duty didn't even lift her head; it was eerie. We walked down the corridors; the people we passed took no notice of us whatsoever. I could only think this was due to Peter and this strange power he had.

The main door of the hospital came into view; it was drizzling. I only had a cardigan on over a sweatshirt. I hoped Peter had some sort of transport. As if reading my mind, Peter said that when we got to the main street I was to hail a taxi. I told him I had no money on me with which to pay for it and if we were travelling ten miles or so it would be pretty expensive.

As we stepped onto the main road, a car travelling at high speed crossed to where we were standing from the other side of the road. We both saw the muzzle of the gun sticking out of the car window at the same time. Peter's reaction was to shove me against the hospital wall. As I fell, I felt a sharp pain in my right shoulder. The car had kept going at high speed and was now disappearing along the road. I looked round to see how Peter had fared from the burst of machine-gun fire that had come from the open window of the car. Peter was nowhere to be seen. I felt sure he must have been hit with the spray of bullets, but he was gone.

A crowd had gathered and some of the hospital staff approached. It was just my luck that of the two nurses present, one was from the ward I had just left. She seemed astonished and was about to say something when they brought a stretcher and carried me to the emergency ward.

On the way I was wondering how to explain all this to everybody. There were going to be a lot of people—doctors, police, and last but not least, my own people—wanting to know how I got into this mess.

The doctor looked at my shoulder. He said the bullet had passed right through it. Just then, the nurse who had been on the road outside came into the room. She pulled the doctor to one side. I could imagine what she was saying to him. This man was a patient in her ward up until just an hour ago. The doctor turned around as if what she had told him was un-believable. He walked back over to where I was lying and lifted the sheet from my legs. He examined both my legs. He then lifted the sheet up to my neck. I could feel him pressing my chest to see if he got any reaction. He got none.

The nurse came over and the doctor turned and asked, "Are you sure this is the same man who was in your ward?"

She said yes. They both went out, closing the curtain.

I looked down at my shoulder and there was nothing; no bullet wound, no blood, nothing, it was as if nothing had happened. I looked up. Standing beside the bed was Peter. My mind couldn't even try to comprehend what was happening. Peter said, "Get your clothes back on and hurry."

I didn't have to be told twice. I knew that there was no way I could explain all this.

Peter pulled the curtain aside. We could see the nurse and doctor talking to two police officers. Peter tugged at my sleeve. We both moved away from where the main group of people were gathered. There was a door farther along the cubicles. Peter opened this and we both found ourselves in some sort of storeroom. There was a door over on the left. I opened it slowly. There was daylight; it was a service entrance for medical supplies.

We both walked along toward a small gate, which was about fifty yards from the main gate. The place was cordoned off. There was a taxi rank and we got into the first taxi. Peter put a handful of paper money into my hand. The driver said, "Where to?"

Peter told the driver the Grange Farm, off the Holmoor Road. The driver knew the road, but not the farm.

"Give me a shout when to stop," he said.

I said okay and looked at Peter; he would have to tell me.

I saw the driver had a paper and asked him if I could see it. He passed it back. I looked at the front page. There would be nothing of today's incident in it, but I might learn more about the crisis Janet had mentioned. The front page had the headlines I was looking for. The Arabs had joined forces against Israel and were threatening to go to war. This was why there was so much activity at the embassies.

Janet had been right about the crisis. If both superpowers got involved, the world could have its final war. Down at the bottom of the page, two names caught my eye, they were Detective Inspector Frazer and Sergeant Morgan. They were both dead, killed in a crash with a heavy goods truck. I looked at Peter. He knew what I had been reading; he said they were killed by the same people who tried to kill us.

I had many questions to ask, but thought I'd better wait until we reached our destination. There was one question that I was afraid to ask, so I had been putting it at the back of my mind. This was, were Peter and his friends the disciples of Jesus? This seemed crazy, but how else could I explain what had happened? The injuries I had received were gone. Peter had appeared and disappeared when it suited him.

I would have it confirmed shortly. We were turning into the Holmoor Road. Peter told me to tell the driver where to stop. It was at an old farm gate, the kind you would see down any country road where there were farms.

We both got out at the gate, and I paid the driver. My heart was pounding at the thought of meeting another two like Peter; I was disconcerted, to say the least. I wondered what part in their plan I was to play.

Peter had opened the gate. I could see the farmhouse from the winding path we were on. It was made of old sandstone instead of the more modern brick. The whitewash on the sandstone looked neglected. As we approached the door of the farmhouse, it opened. The man who appeared was dressed just like Peter. He hugged Peter like you would a long lost brother. My heart was still pounding when Peter introduced us.

"This is John," he said. "John, meet David."

"I like the name," said John. He turned and ushered us into the house.

The front room was bleak; it looked as if it had been lying empty before Peter and his friends had occupied it. The smell of dampness and decay was very strong. John spoke first. "Well, Peter, have you told Mr. Martin anything about what we want him to do?"

Peter smiled and said it was hard enough trying to get me here. "One of the various organizations trying to stop us shot David."

I asked Peter what, or who, these people were. Peter said they knew some of them, but it was becoming confusing as to who else had become involved. I asked if these people knew who they were.

John answered, "Yes, that's part of the problem. They are

afraid of us and what could happen if knowledge of us got about."

I didn't know how that could harm them.

I asked both of them, "Surely these people who are trying to stop what you are trying to do don't know the consequences if you fail?"

Peter was going to pursue this some more when John interrupted. "I'm sorry, David, but we must get on with what's most important now. We would like you to approach Sir George Anders. He has the necessary contacts in the diplomatic sphere. You must convince him, after we have told you the necessary facts, that what you tell him is totally factual and will happen if the correct steps are not taken." I was listening with great interest to what John was saying, but before he could tell me what this information was, the door opened and in stepped this very young-looking man. He was dressed just like John and Peter and had the same tanned face, radiant eyes, shoulder-length hair, and sandals. He had some-one with him. The first man shook hands with both John and Peter.

He turned to me. "You must be David." He said, "My name is Mark. My friend here is called Gorvik."

We shook hands. Peter asked him how his journey had gone.

"Very difficult," he replied. "It's hard trying to get out of Russia at the best of times, but we managed. We have twenty-four hours till Gorvik has to return. If they find out he has been out of the country, the information we give him will be useless.

"He is in the same position you are, Mr. Martin, a junior minister to one of the politburo hierarchy. Who he is does not matter, only what Mr. Gorvik has to tell him, and hopefully he will believe what he is told."

I looked at Gorvik and wondered if he thought or knew

who these people were. By the way he was looking at them, he had come to the same conclusion I had and had had it verified by Mark. It wouldn't take a very high I.Q. to figure out who they were, but it was still very hard to believe.

Peter interrupted my thoughts by saying he would now give Gorvik and myself the information we needed to make this plan successful. First Peter said, "I will tell you what has led to our intervention in this. A crisis will take place between America and Libya. There will be a small exchange of forces in the Gulf of Libya. This exchange will gain world-wide publicity. This in itself won't cause the major crisis, but the action after this has taken place will bring about a major confrontation between America and Russia. As you remember happened when Iran and America were negotiating for the hostages and the talks failed.

"America threatened to take stronger action to release the hostages. They tried a commando-type raid with helicopters, which failed. That's when Russia moved into Afghanistan. The Russians thought at the time they should move first, as a jumping-off base if America should try to invade Iran. As you know, the hostages were eventually freed with help from some of America's friends. This enabled both countries to withdraw from any serious confrontation.

"The crisis that will take place this time will involve not only the superpowers but Third World countries as well. This will come about by their individual loyalty to both America and Russia. The Arab states are uniting against Israel at this precise moment. And as you know, this will involve America further in a conflict in which there will be no winners.

"Your part in this, Mr. Martin, and of course yours, Mr. Gorvik, will be to give your senior ministers a step-by-step account of what will take place before it happens. This information will be written down as we explain it to you."

Peter and Mark did the explaining, while John took

notes. As they came to the end of the information, both Gorvik and I spoke at the same time. Gorvik put his hand out as a gesture that I should speak first. I turned to Peter.

"If all you have told us is true, why don't you and your friends [I still couldn't bring myself to call them disciples] do what's necessary to stop it all happening in the first place? I have no doubt that you have the power to do anything necessary to bring peace before it's too late."

Peter looked at me as he had that time at the hospital, as if I were a little boy who had lost his way and needed help finding it again. "Mr. Martin, it is not for us to interfere in the affairs of mankind. Only when it becomes a situation where man, in his stupidity, seeks to destroy all mankind, even when he thinks it will not come to that. Mankind does not believe anyone will use the weapon that will destroy this planet. He thinks the threat of using it will be sufficient to win his war; by this I mean the powers who have the bomb.

"For us to interfere further than we have would create much the same situation we are trying to avoid."

Peter finished speaking. I couldn't figure out how, if they took a more positive role, it would create the same circumstances they were trying to stop. I was about to voice this when John said, "If you and Mr. Gorvik will bear with us until this crisis is over, the leader of our group will answer all your questions, of which you must have many. We have exactly two weeks to accomplish our task. This is not a lot of time in which to do it, as each day brings ultimate disaster nearer."

Mr. Gorvik and I were the first to leave. Mark went with him. Before leaving, John gave Gorvik a list of the forthcoming events for his minister. He shook my hand and wished me luck. I did the same.

Peter turned to me and gave me the same list. "You shall leave in a half hour, David."

We both left after I said good-bye to John and Mark.

We walked down the path toward the main Holmoor Road. Peter said there was a phone box about fifty yards along the road. I could call a cab from there. I asked if he would be coming with me.

He said, "No, I can't help you from this moment on," as it was up to me to see the plan was carried out as arranged.

The taxi took about fifteen minutes. I shook hands with Peter and thanked him for everything he had done for me. He replied, "Don't worry, David. God's on your side. Good-bye."

The taxi then drove off.

"Where to, mister?" the driver asked.

"Corvine Street," I replied, "near Victoria."

"Okay," he replied.

I felt dirty. The first thing I was going to do was shave and change my clothes. It was funny to think this was still Friday evening; after all that had happened, Sunday seemed a long time ago.

As the taxi approached my house, I looked about the street before getting out. It looked peaceful enough, so I paid the driver and went into the house. The place was in a shambles. Everything was scattered all over the place. Somebody had been busy searching for something. I knew there was nothing to interest anybody, but whoever had ransacked my flat didn't. I tidied the place up, then showered and got dressed. I was feeling hungry. I also felt the need to confide in someone I could trust. Janet came to mind. The phone book was among the papers still scattered about. I decided to phone her house. As it was past six o'clock, she should be finished with her work at the embassy. She answered the phone right away.

"Hello," she said, in her best secretarial voice.

"It's me, David," I said.

"David, where have you been? Are you alright? Where are you?"

"Slow down," I said. "Listen, Janet, I'm okay. I want you to meet me at the Coconut Grove Restaurant. We'll have some dinner and I'll explain everything over dinner."

"Okay," she said, "I'll see you at seven-thirty outside the restaurant."

I got to the restaurant early. I was still wondering if I should tell Janet everything that had happened. When she turned the corner, she looked gorgeous, wearing a light green dress, with matching jacket. Before she could speak, I kissed her on the mouth. As I drew away from her, she started to cry.

"Look," I said, "I'm okay." I didn't think she felt as strongly as this toward me.

I was about to put my arms around her, as a gesture of comfort, when both my arms were grasped at the elbows. I pulled both arms away and swung a fist at the guy to my left. He was too quick for me. He caught my wrist and jerked my arm up my back.

"Look," I said, "who the hell are you?"

Janet said, "Don't hurt him." I told Janet to go. I didn't want her involved and maybe getting hurt. "They're from my embassy," she said. "They had my phone tapped."

Just then a car pulled alongside us and I was bundled into the back. They left Janet standing on the pavement. Now I knew why she had been crying. They had forced her to meet me to make the snatch easier.

"Where are you taking me?"

There were four of them. The biggest of them replied, the American accent plain enough, "Look, Mr. Martin, don't give us any problems and you'll be okay."

I had an idea what they were after, but how could I explain it so they would believe me? I would just have to play it by ear until I was sure.

The big fellow said, "Hood him."

The guy next to me pulled a black hood from his pocket. The other man pulled my arms behind my back and hand-cuffed me. Before the hood went over my head, I noticed we were passing Piccadilly Circus. I pushed upward, as if rising to my feet, but was pulled down with a punch in the guts. But I had achieved my goal, which was to see the mileage on the speedometer.

The hood was pulled roughly over my head. The man on my left who put the hood on clipped my jaw as he took his hand away. I had seen this done in pictures, but this hood was of a heavy material, not the kind they used in pictures. I felt as if I was suffocating. The string at the bottom of the hood was cutting into my throat. I tried to get the front parts of the hood into my mouth quickly; this only created an intense stifling inside the hood.

I decided to try to relax. Before I blacked out, I was listening for anything that might tell me where I was or where I was going. The car slowed to a stop.

"Right, buddy, let's go!"

My arm was pulled up, and I was propelled forward. My foot hit something, and I felt myself falling. My head hit the edge of what felt like a stair. I was half stunned. My shoulder had taken most of the fall on what must have been the step below. I felt the warm blood running down my face.

"You stupid bastard. Why did you push him?"

"He tripped," I heard the other guy say.

"Get him on his feet." The voice belonged to the big guy who had been sitting in the front of the car.

My arms were pulled again, only a little more gently this time. I counted the steps as they led me up. There wasn't much noise, traffic-wise. We had been in the car about half an hour. We could be anywhere outside London, or we could have gone around in circles and be a few miles from where we started. I heard a buzzer being pressed; the door opened. "Take him to the interrogation room; we'll be along shortly."

We walked along what must have been a corridor, for we didn't turn any corners until a door was opened. I was put in a chair and the blindfold taken off. There were two of them standing there. My eyes were becoming adjusted to the dim lights when one of them said, "Better get him some water for his head."

I croaked that I could use a drink as well. My throat felt as though I were on fire.

"Keep your mouth shut until you're asked something, Limey."

By the sound of his voice this was the idiot who'd shoved me when I got out of the car. The other guy came in then. He had a basin and towel. "Loosen his cuffs," the small man said; they hadn't used any names as yet.

The cuffs were taken off and the basin placed on my knees. The water was warm, so there was no way I could drink any. "You better get him something to drink."

I thought I'd ask Chess what this was all about. "Look, Chess, why have you brought me here?"

"Listen, Limey keep your mouth shut or do you want another lump to match that one?"

I got on with washing my face. I felt my forehead. The blood had come from a small cut about a half-inch across; the swelling was worse than the cut by the feel of it.

The small guy came back. "Here," he said. It was a glass of water. He took the basin away. I drank the water without stopping. I felt my throat getting back to something like normal.

The door opened again and the big fellow came in. "Right, you two, out. Leave us alone."

"Okay, sir," came the reply in unison. They left.

"Well, Mr. Martin, I'm sorry for the idiot who shoved you.

That wasn't supposed to happen. We've brought you here because we want to know why or how you're involved in all this."

"In all what?" I replied.

"Let me finish first, Mr. Martin. You were the recipient of a phone call last Sunday. You were to meet someone at the pub that was bombed. One of our own people was there, he was killed in the blast.

"You were then taken to the hospital, from which you managed to elude not only the hospital staff but police and some other people who were keeping an eye on you.

"That wasn't the end, Mr. Martin. You were then shot at from a car as you tried to leave the hospital. You were supposed to have been shot, according to our source, but as with everything else that's supposed to have been done to you, we think it's all a prefabrication for something else."

They seemed to know most of the facts, but I felt he hadn't told me everything he knew about the phone call.

"That's easy, Mr. Martin; we have your phone tapped."

"I thought you people were supposed to be our allies?" I said.

"Well, we're in the business of security, Mr. Martin. After the Philby affair, we don't take chances in letting Russia have a free hand in our joint affairs."

"Do your people know that you're tapping their phones?"

"This isn't getting us anywhere, David."

This was the first time he had used my first name. "We want to know who helped you at the hospital and where you went after you gave us all the slip."

"Well," I said, "you seem to know my name; what's yours?"

"Just call me Mr. H., David; that will do for now."

"Okay, Mr. H., I got the phone call you mentioned. This could get kind of confusing unless you've read the Bible. Mr.

H., I'm afraid even if you have, you're not going to believe me."

"Try me, Mr. Martin."

I told him everything I knew, except two things: Gorvik and a list of what was to happen in the next two weeks.

"You expect me to believe this crap you're giving me? Look, Martin, I want straight answers from you or I send in that arsehole who did that to your head."

"I told you you wouldn't believe me," I said.

"Okay, Martin, have it your way."

At that he crossed to the door and pressed a button. The door opened and in came Chess and his sidekick. "Look," H. said, "this Limey's giving me the runaround. See if you can get any sense from him."

"It will be a pleasure, sir."

"Don't make it show, okay?"

"Right, sir."

H. left.

"Okay, Limey, are you going to cooperate, or do we convince you the hard way? Cuff him!"

The small guy took the handcuff out of his pocket and walked around behind me.

Well, I thought, *if these two are going to work me over, I'll get the first blow in before I'm handcuffed.*

Chess was standing over me grinning like a Cheshire cat. That's when I shoved the chair back and caught the little guy by the shins with the rung of the chair. A split second after this, I brought my feet up into Chess's groin. He toppled like a felled tree. I ran for the door, but this time the short one had recovered from the pain in his shins. His tackle would have done him proud on any rugby team. We both slid along the floor and hit the wall. He still had hold of my feet. I turned and let him have a few mouthfuls of leather. He didn't look

20

too pleased, especially with the gap that appeared where his teeth had been.

I could see King Kong getting up from the floor. The look on his face was enough to tell me my time was up. He came across and pulled his mate out of the way. His big hand grabbed me by the tie. I felt the first two blows, after that I blacked out.

I don't know how long I was out. When I woke up, I was lying on the floor, still handcuffed. I couldn't see my watch, so I didn't know how much time had gone by. There were no windows in the room. It could have still been night or another day. If it was Sunday, it would be okay. The first event on the paper Peter had given me was to happen on Monday.

My body was aching. Chess must have had a ball while I was out for the count. I managed to get to my feet. The door was locked. I didn't expect it to be open; these guys were too careful. The chair was still there, so I sat down, wondering what would happen next.

I must have dozed off. The door opening awakened me. It was Janet.

"How the hell did you get here?" I said.

"Leave that till later," she said.

I was all for that, just to get me out of there.

"Follow me," she said. "Keep it quiet."

We went out the door and along the corridor. There were two doors. One was slightly ajar. I could hear them talking. Janet turned and pointed to the far end of the corridor. We crept past the door where the voices came from.

At the bottom of the corridor we turned left. Janet whispered, "This is the back entrance to the safe house."

We both went out into what was the back alley. "Hurry," she said, "before they check the interrogation room."

The main road looked clear enough. "My car is two blocks

21

away," she added. "I had to leave it and walk here, just in case they were watching the road."

"Okay, Janet, how did you find me?"

"Easy," she said. "I'm the secretary at the embassy, remember? I got the list of safe houses and drove around until one showed signs of life."

"Good girl, now where do we go from here?"

"I've taken the keys to one of the safe houses. You can stay there until you explain all this to me."

I said, "Great. What time is it?"

"One o'clock in the morning," she replied.

"Sunday morning?" I asked.

"Of course," she said, looking at me as if I had gone senile.

We got to the car in a couple of minutes. "You don't have a key to these handcuffs, by any chance," I asked.

"I'm good, David, but not that good."

I smiled at this; she had a good sense of humor.

TWO

We arrived at the safe house at two o'clock. I was surprised by the safe house. It had everything. Janet lit the fire, which was one of those false log fires with gas heating. I flopped down on the big easy chair facing the fire. I was sore and tired, but I would have to ask Janet some questions. First I asked if there was a tool cupboard, so I could get these damned handcuffs off. Janet found some tools in the basement cellar. She brought up a small hacksaw and various other tools.

"The hacksaw will do," I said. I knelt down in front of her and saw the chain links. They'd be easier to break than the solid metal.

It took Janet half an hour to cut through the single chain link. She cut her fingers a few times in the effort. My hands were now free. The first thing I did was give Janet a hug and kiss. "That was painful," I said. "The big fellow sure knew how to hit where it hurt most." My lips were swollen and my chest was bruised. He must have stuck the boot in a few times after I was knocked out.

"How do you feel?" Janet asked.

"Rough," I said. "Look, Janet, I'll have to wash and then tell you what I know."

I felt better after I had bathed. Janet was waiting with a steaming mug of coffee.

"Thanks, Janet. I need this."

"Right, David. How about telling me what's going on?"

"Okay, Janet, but like your countrymen it's going to be hard to believe. Remember when I was taken to the hospital after the explosion, I was supposed to have broken my leg and cracked ribs?"

She nodded.

"Well, I don't have them now, do I? The same goes for the bullet that's supposed to have gone through my shoulder. This was all due to a man called Peter." Now came the hard part. How do you tell someone the person you're talking about is, or you think he is, one of the disciples out of the Bible?

After ten minutes I had finished telling Janet the story so far. She looked at me as if the blows the big man had given me had unhinged my brain.

"Well, Janet, I told you it was going to sound far-fetched."

She said, "Far-fetched is putting it mildly; are you sure all this has happened the way you say it has? Couldn't it be induced through drugs or some form of hypnosis?"

"You tell me," I said. "It's as real to me as these bruises are."

"You mentioned they gave you a list of what was to happen in the next two weeks?"

"I just remembered your countrymen may have searched me. Look in my inside pocket of my jacket!"

"It's here," Janet said.

"Let me see it, Janet. I think the first event in the letter happens tomorrow."

We both looked at the list; the first item was to do with the French government. They were going to conduct excursions into Libya to protect their interests in Chad. The first incident would take place at ten o'clock Monday morning.

"That's tomorrow," Janet said. "What are you going to do?"

"I'm supposed to contact my boss and convince him that what I say is the truth. Look, Janet, how much do you know about your people's involvement in all this?"

24

"Very little, David, just what you've told me and what's taken place since last night."

"Do you think you can get any information from your embassy?"

"I'll try, David, but it's not easy. I'm not privy to all that's going on."

"Be careful, Janet; they may suspect you of having something to do with my disappearance. Will they miss the set of keys for this place?"

"No, I'll put them back tomorrow when I go into work, or should I say in a couple of hours. What will you do, David?"

"I'll try to contact Sir George."

"Be careful, David."

"I'll be alright, Janet."

I looked at the clock; it was four o'clock. "Why don't you stay here, Janet, and go in to the embassy in the morning?"

"No, David, it's too dangerous. They may be watching my house. I'll have to sneak in the back way. They won't think of looking for you here, David, not one of their own safe houses." She put her coat on and collected the keys from the sideboard. "I'll take this number and phone later, David."

"No," I said, "they may have this place tapped even though it's their own house. Meet me at Marble Arch at seven tonight. There's a small door at the side; just push it and come up the stairs. I used to play there as a youngster. It'll be okay." I got up from the chair and kissed her, "I'll put the light out before I open the door." She kissed me again and was gone.

I was very tired. A few hours' sleep would help me think straight.

I woke at one in the afternoon. I was still feeling sore and stiff, but after some breakfast I felt better. Now I had to figure out what my next move was to be. Getting Sir George on a Sunday afternoon would be quite a feat, as I didn't know his whereabouts on week-ends, especially on Sunday. I couldn't

25

phone him from here, and I had no transport. As I looked about me, I noticed a set of keys. They were Janet's; she must have left them intentionally. Good girl! I could drive to Sir George's home. Before I left I opened a back window slightly, having no keys to get back in. If I made it back the window would be sufficient for entry. I left a list of future happenings in a safe place, I only hoped the boss would listen to what I said and believe me.

On my way to Sir George's, my thoughts went back to what Janet said about me being drugged or receiving some other form of autosuggestion. This didn't seem possible to me—the two detectives who were killed in the road accident weren't killed by bad driving. Someone had planned their so-called accident. That's when it came to me that the paper could prove part of my story by having the two detectives' names in the paper. But that in itself wouldn't convince Sir George my story was true. I could only hope the first incident on the list would convince him otherwise.

"What happened, Harry?"

"Martin managed to get out of the safe house sir. We believe he had inside help; nobody knew where we had him, except his girlfriend at the embassy. She hasn't turned up for work yet. We're watching her flat. Martin gave us some cock-and-bull story about disciples and the reason why they're here. He tried to escape, and Chess gave him a going over. If you could give us more information on what it is he's supposed to have done, we would be able to maybe make more progress."

"I'm sorry, Harry; I can't say any more than it's imperative that you find him before the Russians do."

"The Russians! How do they come into this?"

"We've just got intelligence reports that they want Martin just as much as we do. Harry, send the report on that story Martin told you about disciples, etc."

"Okay, sir, I'll get it to the code room within the hour."

Harry put the phone down and switched off the phone scrambler. "Bloody bastards won't give us any more information on what Martin's supposed to know . . . anything on that secretary yet, Chester?"

"Nothing, Harry. It's as if she's still with Martin. We're trying to trace her car. We told the police it's been stolen; that might help if they come up with something."

"What about you Louie?"

"I've been checking all Martin's known haunts, but nobody's seen or heard anything."

"Right. Get some more men onto this. The two buddies Martin works with and his boss, Sir George Anders, have them watched in case Martin tries to contact them. Have their phones been tapped?"

"Yes," Chess said. "Anders wasn't too easy. That's some mansion he's got and bloody hard to get into. Did you know they've got two plainclothesmen walking the grounds in case some IRA nutter tries to bump him off?"

"Yes, I know; they all have them. I'll get this report to the code room; then we'll get to hell out and maybe get lucky. Oh, Louie, before we go, did you check the secretary's desk?"

"Yes," Louie said, "nothing of interest there."

"What about the keys to the safe houses?"

"I forgot about them," said Louie.

"Well, move your arse and check them out. That secretary's no dummy; she could have thought of using them."

I arrived at Sir George's house, or should I say mansion— this place was big! As I drove up the driveway a man stepped out of the bushes to my left and began waving me down. I stopped and he came round to the driver's side of the car.

"Hello. I'm here to see Sir George."

"Step out of the car if you don't mind, sir."

I'd forgot that Sir George had twenty-four-hour security, as nearly all government ministers had. I got out of the car, and the man told me to put my hands on top of the car bonnet and spread my legs. He frisked me for weaponry I might have been carrying. When he found none, I turned around.

"Do you have any form of identification, sir?" While looking at it he asked what I wanted Sir George for.

"I work for Sir George at the ministry and have something important which he should know about."

"Come with me, sir."

We then began walking up to the house. He didn't take me to the front entrance, but round the side, and we entered what must have been the servants' entrance. Inside the house he escorted me to a small room off the main corridor.

When we entered there was another man sitting, sipping a cup of tea or coffee.

"Keep an eye on Mr. Martin, Sid, till I see the governor," my pal said before leaving.

"Okay, Junior. Sit down, Mr. Martin."

"Thanks, Sid. Sorry about this but it's procedure."

"That's okay."

"Do you want a cup of coffee?"

"Yes please."

The coffee was just at my lips when Junior appeared. "Sir George will see you in his study, Mr. Martin. I'll show you where it is."

We went up a flight of stairs, then through half a dozen doors before we got to the study.

Junior knocked on the door.

The reply was immediate. "Come in!"

Junior entered first; the slight nod from Sir George must have meant I was who I said I was. Junior left.

Sir George was standing over a blazing log fire. In one hand he had a drink; with the other he waved me to a chair.

"Well, David, where have you been these past few days? The police and security have been looking for you; they seem to think you know more than you've been telling them."

"Well, Sir George, I don't know how they came to that conclusion. I haven't spoken to anyone about it."

"What about the Americans?"

The look on my face must have been strange, for Sir George started laughing. "Don't look so surprised, David. The Americans aren't the only ones who can decipher codes."

"I'm sorry, Sir George; I was going to tell you about that."

"That's okay, David. Why don't you start at the beginning? Take your time."

When I had finished, Sir George sat down. He looked at me and asked, "Let me see your leg and chest."

I showed him my leg.

"That's the one that's supposed to have been broken, is it?"

I nodded. I pulled up my shirt and he asked if those bruises were from the pub bombing.

"No, they were put there by our American friends when they kidnapped me."

"Where is the list of events that they said they had given you?"

"I only brought one, sir." I handed him the paper on which I had written the first prediction.

"Where's the rest of the predications?"

"In a safe place."

"Why didn't you bring all of them?"

"They said to tell you one event at a time."

"So tomorrow morning at ten o'clock the French will invade Libya?"

"Yes."

"Do you believe that, David?"

29

"I don't know, sir. So much has happened in the last week."

"I feel as if this has happened to me, and it feels real."

"Are you going to take any action to prevent this event from occurring, sir?"

"Well, David, you have to admit it sounds a bit far-fetched. The disciple part, I mean, if I was to believe you I'm going to need more than this to stick my neck out. Could you see me trying to explain this to the prime minister? She might believe the French bit, because we have been expecting the French to do this for some time to save their interest in Chad. But this other thing about the second coming, as I would call it, there's just no chance of me telling her about it without her thinking I should be locked up."

"We've only got ten days, sir, and if they're correct none of us will have to worry who believes what."

"Look, David, can't you get something more tangible with which I can work?"

"I don't think I can, sir, until the next event."

"Look, David I'll give you two questions to ask these so-called disciples."

"What kind of questions, sir?"

"Just stay there. I'll be back shortly."

While Sir George was away, my mind was running over what I should do next. Time was marching on, and I had to meet Janet at Marble Arch just two hours from now. I hoped Sir George wouldn't be long, but he came back in half an hour.

"Well, David, get me the answer to these two questions and maybe I can begin to believe your story." Then he handed me a sheet of paper with two questions. Before I looked at it, he asked what I was going to do about the people who were looking for me. "My own security may have reported your whereabouts to MI6."

"I hadn't thought of that. Do you think I'll get to my car, sir?"

"Go to the front door, David, wait until I've called them in on the hand radio, then get to your car."

"Thanks, sir."

"Good luck, David." At that he shoved some money into my hand and pushed me out the door.

It took me five minutes to find the front door. I had taken a wrong turn coming out of the study.

I opened the door slowly. The grounds looked clear. I sprinted to the car, shoved the keys in, and went down the drive in reverse. I swung left at the bottom and headed straight for London. I had half an hour to make the rendezvous with Janet. I hoped the police wouldn't pull me over for speeding.

At ten to seven I left the car some distance from where the meeting was, in case Janet had been followed. The Cumberland Hotel was just across the road from Marble Arch. I stood there for five minutes making sure no one was there who shouldn't be.

The place looked clear of any would-be intelligence operators. Janet came into view just below the arch. Not bad timing. It had just gone seven. She was standing at the small door. The bloody thing had been changed; where there used to be a small padlock was changed to a mortise lock. No way we could get in here. We'd better move to another location.

Janet looked tired and drawn. I kissed her, saying, "You look as if you haven't slept for a week."

"Thanks," she said, "but I haven't since the time I left you at the safe house. When I left you to go home my place was being watched. I went round the back, but that was covered as well, then I decided not to go to work either."

"Listen, let's try for a room across at the Cumberland Hotel."

I took her hand and we ran across when the traffic slowed

to a crawl. I'd been in the Cumberland before when meeting some minor dignitary from Arabia. It was used by the Arabs when they were over here more than any other hotel in London.

As we approached the desk, the clerk said, "Yes, sir?" meaning, of course, "What do you want?"

I sort of stuttered and asked for "a single room, please," turning to Janet. She smiled, knowing why I had stuttered.

"Name please?"

"Oh, Mr. and Mrs. Roberts."

Janet laughed, and the clerk looked at us with one of those know-it-all faces.

"Your keys, sir. Do you have any luggage?"

"No," I replied. "It's following after."

I pulled Janet toward the stairway. We got room 34. She was still laughing when I closed the room door.

"Well?" I said.

"I was thinking of you, my Sir Galahad." Another fit of laughter.

"Right, Janet. Finish what you were telling me."

"As the house was being too well watched for me to go home, I've been wandering the streets with the occasional stop for coffee. I think I've been to every cafe in London."

"You didn't go near the embassy then?"

"No, I was too scared. How did you get on with Sir George?"

"Look, before we start on that, let's get something to eat." I called down and ordered steaks with french fries and a pot of coffee.

After we had gorged ourselves, I told Janet to go and get herself some clothes, as there was a cheap clothier just outside the hotel. The money Sir George had given me amounted to £250.

I gave Janet £50. "Take the keys, Janet. I'll take a bath while you're gone."

By the time she came back I'd had my bath. Janet showed me what she had got for her £50—two pairs of jeans, some underclothes, and a v-neck jumper. "Is there a shower room?" she asked.

"Yes, through there." I pointed. I ordered more coffee for when she came out.

The coffee had just arrived when Janet came out of the bathroom. She looked stunning—the tight-fitting jeans clinging to her figure, the v-necked jumper showing she had left her bra off.

She laughed. "Is it that bad?" she asked.

"No," I said, spilling my coffee. My heart was pounding.

She sat down beside me and poured herself a coffee. "I've got some washing in the bath, David; do you have anything you want washed?" Her skin was glowing. "Are you listening to me, David?"

"Yes, I'm sorry, Janet; you just look so beautiful. I love you."

"Thanks, David." Then she was in my arms and she was crying.

"What's wrong, Janet?" I asked, wiping the tears away from her cheek.

"I'm afraid. What are we going to do, David?"

"Don't worry, love. Sir George won't let me down."

"Then he believed what you told him?"

"Well, not exactly. He's given me two questions for Peter. If the answers are what Sir George thinks are true, he will believe the rest of the story."

"What are the questions?"

"I've not looked at the paper myself."

I took the paper out of my pocket, and we both read it. The first question was. "Is Charles Darwin's theory of evolution of man true? If not, what is the truth of man's evolution from apes?"

"You would think Sir George could find some better question than that," said Janet.

"Not if the answer can clear up something which has contradicted everything that Western countries believe is the truth of the Bible," I replied. "Darwin's theory of evolution has caused arguments since he published his book. He had to defend his theory to the church and to the establishment. My own thoughts are in agreement with Darwin, as it has been proved by scientists that all animals are descendents of one type of prehistoric animal or other and all originated from the sea. We know Darwin's theory to be correct on the evolution of animals. If the answer I get from Peter contradicts this theory, it will have to be good for me to be able to convince Sir George and whomever he gives this information to as well.

"If Darwin's theory is correct on the origin of man, then the Bible is wrong in more ways than one and this would create a disbelief in the Bible from the start to finish. I only hope Peter has the right answers to convince them."

I turned to Janet. Her face had gone an ashen colour. What I had been saying had affected her profoundly.

"But what if he's right, David? It would destroy the hopes and beliefs of millions. The corruption and evil that go on would triple overnight."

"That's true, Janet. People with very little to lose would go over the edge and do things they wouldn't normally do."

"What about the other question?"

"It concerns the dinosaurs—why did they all die at the same time?"

"Well, that's something similar to the last one. All the dinosaurs seemed to die off at the same time. What caused this has never been fully explained, though there's plenty of theories.

"A giant meteorite hitting earth and blocking out the sun, with after effects, something like that would happen if we had a nuclear war and the earth went into another ice age. Simply by the refuse thrown round the earth and blocking out the sun all the plant and animal life would perish, including us. There are many theories, but that's all they are. The real question Sir George is asking is, Was man around the time they perished? If the answer is no, that knocks the Bible on the head."

"How does it do that, David?"

"If man wasn't around then, the Bible would be wrong in the creation of the earth in seven days and man's creation shortly after, and if there was a change in the earth around that time, how did man survive? I don't think Sir George thought these questions up; they are not something he would be too well onto. He must have contacted someone when he left me in the study. The only thing now is, How do I get in contact with Peter or any of the other disciples?

"Well, Janet, I'll take the couch and you take the bed." I was talking to myself. Janet had dropped off with her head resting against the couch. I got up and laid her out straight; she was breathing gently. I kissed her forehead and put the light out. I was pretty bushed myself. I called down for an alarm call at 7 A.M., then went to sleep.

THREE

When David left the house and Sir George called the two security men in so he could get away without being seen, he asked the two men if they had contacted their department.

Sid replied that what they had done was the usual procedure. "Where is Martin now?"

"He is gone, Sid; didn't you see him leave?"

Before he could answer, they heard Martin's car drive away. "Excuse me, sir," and Junior shot out the door.

"He will be too late to catch him, I'm afraid, Sid."

"You knew we were after him, sir; why did you allow him to go?"

"For reasons which I can't go into just now; you will have to take my word for it. Of course you can tell your superiors what I've told you."

"I will, Sir George."

Junior came in then. "He's well away, Sid. Get onto Control and tell them, say we think he's heading for London and Sir George helped him elude us. You can both go back to your normal duty."

Sid was going to say something, but the look Sir George gave him made him change his mind.

"Hello, Prime Minister, Sir George Anders here. . . . I've just had a visit from my junior minister. . . . Yes, the one who was in the bombing, etc. I have allowed him to go. You will probably get a call from the head of security; they have been notified by their people stationed here. I will take full responsibility for this and give you a full report on Monday morning.

". . . Thank you, Prime Minister. I think it was necessary. . . . Good-bye."

Sir George poured himself a drink and sat down thinking of young Martin's story. The lad either was off his rocker or had been got at by someone. The story he told was just too far-fetched to be believed. *Though I couldn't try to work out how his injuries were so mysteriously cleared up,* Sir George wondered. The doctors who examined Martin at the hospital confirmed he had the injuries, which were no longer visible. The bullet wound was also confirmed. The man should have been dead by now, but he wasn't. There was no reasonable explanation for his recovery; his story of disciples and why they were here could be given credence by his own recovery from the injuries.

Why the Americans should want to get him was a further mystery. *Did they believe his story?* Sir George wondered. *If so, why? They either had more information than us or knew the true story about what was going on and hadn't bothered to ask us for help to resolve it. As Martin was a British subject and part of the government, though in a small way, they must realize this could lead to a diplomatic incident, which would lead to both countries going onto the defensive as far as intelligence sharing was concerned.*

Britain and America had always been close when it came to this cooperation, though the Philby case had knocked them back a few years. *They must be very worried if they are doing it without consulting us. I only hope I took the right decision in allowing David to go,* Sir George wondered. *The phone call to Professor Links to find out what he would ask if he had a chance to speak with one of Jesus' disciples. . . . The professor sort of laughed; then he asked me why I'd called. We were old friends from our college days. "Oh," I said, "we were sitting at home with some friends when we got onto the topic of religion, and this question arose, which I'm putting to you. We were curious to find out what a prominent professor of religion would ask a disciple. He then proceeded to give me two questions, which would, as he put it, end the speculation over Darwin's theory of*

37

evolution and why all the dinosaurs disappeared at nearly the same time. This, he said, would give more answers to whether there was a God or not. He explained a little more and then I thanked him and hung up.

I couldn't see at the time why he chose these questions, but the more I thought about them, the clearer they became. These two questions would unlock the door to many unanswered questions, about man and our planet. They were not the ones I would have expected from the professor. Any other questions could be fobbed off, with the Bible or some other excuse as an answer. With these two questions the answers would have to have some substance, which could be proved. Well, enough pondering to the maybes. Tomorrow would be a big day one way or the other. David's prediction and my explanation to the prime minister about it all will keep me busy. At that Sir George went to the sideboard, had one more scotch, and went to bed.

The phone rang at 7 o'clock precisely. I got up and went through to see if Janet had heard it. She was sitting on the settee rubbing her eyes. "Sorry about falling asleep on you last night."

"You didn't miss much."

She laughed.

"I'll phone down for some breakfast; then we better think what our next move will be."

We had bacon, eggs, and some coffee.

Janet asked, "What's your plan for today?"

I didn't want to sound worried, so I told Janet she should go back to her job.

She said, "How can I? They will want to know the facts about where I was and where you are."

"Don't worry about me; they won't get to me through you. Tell them everything you know. I won't be anywhere they can find me with what you tell them."

"But what are you going to do?"

"Leave that to me, Janet. The less you know the better.

"Go to the embassy after twelve o'clock. That way, the first event will have happened. You can tell them all the story; they won't believe you, the same as they didn't believe me. The event will be in the afternoon papers, so they will surmise you found out that way and you will still be telling them the truth."

"How will I be able to contact you, David?"

"Don't. I'll be in touch with you somehow. I can't stay here; my money's running kind of short."

"I could get you some."

"No, it's too risky. They will have covered that eventually. Just do as I said."

As I got up to get ready to go, there were tears in her eyes. I went to her and held her to me. "Don't worry, love. If it's all true we couldn't have better friends," meaning, of course, the disciples, if I wasn't wrong.

I left. It was half past eight. I paid the bill, which left me with about a hundred-odd pounds; it would have to do. My first step was to see if I could get hold of Peter. The only place I knew of was the farmhouse on the Holmoor road. Then it dawned on me that the rest of the predictions were back at the American safe house; they would have to wait.

The taxi pulled up about two hundred yards before the farmhouse. I didn't want to take any chances in case it was being watched by anyone looking for me. Janet wouldn't have left the hotel yet, so the chances of them knowing about the farmhouse were slight.

I cut through the field to the right of the house; all seemed quiet enough. There were no lights showing. I pushed the door and it opened. That could mean someone was still here or it had been left unlocked intentionally. Well, here goes. I rushed in. I gave myself a fright by falling over a chair near the door. I jumped up, rubbing my chin, as it had taken the force of the blow. It looked deserted. If anyone were there, they would have shown themselves by now.

As I turned to leave, a voice said, "Mr. Martin."

I swung round, startled.

"It's me, Mr. Martin."

"Gorvik, bloody hell, you gave me a turn there!"

Gorvik came out of the shadows, a gun in his hand. He looked as if he had just done a stint on some assault course. His clothes were filthy, and there were some cuts and bruises on his face.

"How did you get here?"

"That's a long story, Mr. Martin."

"Cut out the 'Mr. Martin' bit; David will do. Now what happened? Start from the beginning."

Before he could say anything, the door burst open and two men came in at a run, the first with a gun in his hand. Then a shot rang out. It was Gorvik. Whether through nerves or just being afraid, he had fired at the first guy through the door. He didn't miss. The guy went down in a heap, his partner still running behind him and reaching inside his jacket for what could only be another gun, but before he could draw it, he ended in a heap on his fallen partner. I turned and looked at Gorvik just to make sure he wasn't going to fire again. I needn't have bothered. Gorvik was in shock at what he had already done, I moved fast and grabbed a small rolling pin that was lying on the table, as the second intruder was trying to untangle himself. Before he could get to his feet or draw his gun, I thumped him on the head with the old rolling pin. It broke on his skull but did the job.

The other guy was dead. While I was searching the unconscious one I shouted to Gorvik to search the other one. He came out of his trance and started to look through his victim's pockets.

"What are we looking for, David?"

40

"Anything that will tell us whom they were sent by." I was right about him reaching for a gun—he had a shoulder holster. I put the gun in my jacket pocket. "Get his gun while you're searching him, Gorvik. These are American agents; they still had their ID's. These two weren't the ones who had me the other night."

"Right."

"Gorvik, let's get to hell out of here; they may have friends nearby."

This had all happened within three minutes. Out the door all seemed quiet enough, as we both ran for the hedges on our left.

I looked over the hedge. The car which the two men had come in was parked about fifty yards down the road. "Come on, Gorvik." I grabbed Gorvik's shoulder and pulled him to his feet, I led him to the car. There was no one inside, and the bloody keys weren't in it. "Stay here, Gorvik." I rushed back to the house; the keys were lying with the rest of the stuff from their pockets. I took the keys and, as an afterthought, their identity passes as well; they might come in handy. Gorvik was already sitting in the car. I jumped in the driver's side and headed back to London.

Gorvik told me his story of why he had come back. He said the disciples had nothing to do with him coming back; his own people had found out that he had left the country for some reason and were about to question him on the reason. He had overheard his superiors talking to the KGB. His situation was similar to mine. Phone taps and other intelligence work had led back to him, plus some backstabbing from his friends. If he had stayed they would have made him talk and they would have killed him after he told them all he knew.

"I know the feeling, Gorvik."

"What shall we do now, David?"

41

I then put him in the picture of what had happened to me and what I was doing at the farmhouse. He said he had done the same trying to contact John, but hadn't enough time to wait around. He had bribed a seaman to get aboard a fishing vessel that would call at some port in the north of Scotland. He had then got a train to London and came straight to the farmhouse.

"Well, Gorvik, as I've told you, Janet may have told her own people about everything. I think that's how those two goons came to the farmhouse. The hotel is out; they will be watching there. I've got an idea but it's tricky."

When we reached London I headed for the safe house Janet had got me to. I took the car as near the safe house as was possible, then parked it in a alleyway out of sight. We were about six blocks away from the safe house. I told Gorvik what I was going to do. "There is a small cafe two blocks from the house. You go in and wait till I come back for you, Gorvik; have a cup of tea or something." I left Gorvik at the cafe.

The street looked deserted but for one car parked on the opposite side of the safe house. There were two men in the car. I went round to the back of the house; it looked clear enough. The back window was still open.

That's when a shot rang out. It came from the main street. It was Gorvik and the two in the car, he had followed me and walked right into them. Who fired first I don't know, but one of the men was lying in the middle of the road, a pool of blood forming around his head. Gorvik was lying facedown, not moving. The other man was still at the car, crouched behind the car door. I was still hidden from his view. We both turned to where the sound of a siren was coming from. He ran to where his partner had fallen, put both arms under his comrade, and dragged him to his car, pushing the body into the backseat of the car.

The siren was getting closer. I would have to make my own mind up as to what I was going to do next. The car drove off. I ran to where Gorvik was lying. He had been shot in the shoulder and was still alive. People were beginning to appear from their houses and places of work. The whole thing had happened in the space of five minutes. I would have to leave Gorvik. The police car was entering the main street a block away. I got up and ran for the corner of the safe house. Two people were approaching Gorvik from a small workplace farther along the street. Gorvik would be alright for a little while, I told myself. It would be of little use the both of us being dragged in by the police; that would help no one.

I made for the back of the safe house, climbed over the small wall, and entered the open window. I went to the front of the house and looked out between the curtains. The police were there; one was putting something under Gorvik's head while the other was calling someone on his car radio. The ambulance arrived five minutes later. The police were questioning the people who had been standing about. No one pointed in this direction, so I hoped no one had seen me sneak in here. I would have a couple of hours before anyone came near the place. The police had cordoned the street off, which was the usual procedure while they looked for evidence of the crime.

I collected the ten predictions, sat down, and read them over. If they came true, the world was in for a shaky time up until the last prediction came about, when there wouldn't be any world left to be worried about. Nuclear war was the last prediction, and that was to take place at twelve noon on the sixteenth of June. This was the seventh of June. Nine days' time. I would have to get hold of the paper and see how the first prediction had fared.

My main problem was getting hold of Peter so I could put

Sir George's question to him. Right now a few hours' sleep wouldn't go amiss; it would be a busy night later on.

It was three hours later, to be exact, when the police knocked on the door; they left after about two minutes of knocking and getting no reply. I washed and shaved. You had to hand it to the Americans—they knew how to stock up with the necessities of life. You could stay here for a month without having to leave for supplies. I collected the things I would need for tonight, car keys, gun, the American identification passes. I would try to contact Janet, as I would need her help later.

It was ten past five. Janet would be finishing in just over half an hour. That's if they were still allowing her to carry on at the embassy as usual. They may have decided she was too much of a security risk. I had to hope they hadn't. I looked out of the back window before opening it. I could see people moving up and down the side street. I climbed out of the window and moved up to the wall of the garden. I waited until it was clear of people on the right hand side of the wall. I couldn't see the left hand side, as the wall jutted out slightly on that side. I jumped when I thought it was clear.

Scarcely two yards from where I landed was a policeman, coming from the blind side of the wall. He grabbed my arm. "Excuse me, sir," he said, "but what are you doing?" he had his right hand on my shoulder.

I swung with my right hand straight to his jaw. I was sorry I had to do it, but time wasn't exactly on my side. He went down without a sound. By this time half a dozen people were walking on both sides of the street and some had started to shout. I ran across the road without looking back. This guy tried to stop me by holding his arms widespread; I shouldered him to the ground. I didn't stop. Soon no one was chasing me. I must have run about three blocks from where I had started, and my breath was coming in gulps. I looked up at the street name, James Street, which was just off Oxford Street. There should be a pub on the left hand side. . . there was. I tidied myself up as best as I could and entered the bar. It was crowded, and this was what I needed till things calmed down.

I shouted to the barmaid for a pint of lager. My throat was parched from running, and it tasted delicious. Someone got up to leave, and I grabbed the seat. The car was only a short distance from here.

I relaxed a bit. Life was becoming a bit hectic. Who would have thought I would be hitting policemen and nearly killing people with a kitchen rolling pin? I had to smile. If I was right and failed in what I had to do, all these people and the rest of the world would just be a memory. I glanced at the clock on the pub wall, half past five. There was a phone in the corner of the bar; I could phone Janet from here. I would need some excuse so if the phone was tapped they wouldn't know who it was, who was calling.

I had an idea. I wrote the number down, then called the barmaid over.

She said, "Yes, sir?"

"I wonder if you could do me a favour. Would you call this number for me and ask my fiancée to meet me here when she finishes work?"

"You're joking," she said.

"No, you don't understand. You see, if I call her the telephonist will pull her leg about it; so will other workmates— a private joke, you see. But only if I call her. That's why I'm asking you, please."

"Okay, love, I'll call her, but it better not be a leg pull on me."

"Honest it isn't. Here's the number; tell her it's Mr. Roberts. Her name's Janet Blair."

The barmaid got through right away and asked for Janet.

She did as I had told her and turned to me and said, "She said she'll be here at six-forty, okay?"

"Thanks," I said and leaned over and gave her a kiss.

"I'll have to do that more often," she said, laughing.

I ordered myself another lager. The bar was becoming less crowded as those who had come after work made their way home. I kept my eyes on the door just in case they happened to look for me here. At half past six, I got up and went to the door. There was a public toilet just outside the pub. I walked across and stood by the entrance. If Janet had been followed, I wanted to be sure I didn't walk into a trap as had happened the last time.

I saw Janet turn the corner from the Oxford Street end of James Street. I let her get inside the pub and gave it five minutes before I followed her in. There didn't seem to be anyone who looked like they were following Janet. She was standing at the bar; it looked like she had ordered herself a tomato juice. She was looking round when I entered.

She put her glass down and came toward me, put her arms round my neck, and kissed me. "Oh, David, I was so worried about you. I heard about the shooting; they're all talking about it at the embassy. That's two of their men been killed in one day. I just knew you were involved, weren't you?"

"Yes, I was involved, Janet. I didn't kill anyone, just knocked one of your people unconscious. Gorvik killed the other two."

"Gorvik, how did he get here?"

"That's a long story, Janet. I've got more important things to tell you, and I want some information on which hospital they took Gorvik to and is he still alive."

"Okay, David, I'll tell you what I know about it. They've taken Gorvik to St. Mary's Hospital. He's not too badly wounded. The police are waiting to question him, and our people are hovering around in the background. They haven't told the police they were involved but want to know who Gorvik is and how he's involved in all this. As far as I know, Gorvik hasn't spoken to anyone yet."

I was about to tell Janet what I wanted her to do for me when she said, "I haven't finished yet, David. I've got something important to tell you. Two of my people want to speak to you."

I jumped up. "What? Do they know I'm here, talking to you?"

"Yes, David. Don't panic; they won't come unless I send for them."

I sat down again. "How do you know you can trust them, Janet?"

"These two have come from the president of the United States."

"How do you know they're not just playing you along to get to me?" I said.

"Because, believe it or not, the president spoke to me on the phone at the embassy. The conversation couldn't be overheard, as it was made on the president's special phone to the embassy, which isn't bugged."

I sat there stupefied and mystified. "Why does the president want to see you? Better still, how does he even know I exist?"

"I don't have the answers to those questions, David. These two agents might be able to answer them if you agree to see them."

"When is this meeting to take place?"

"I've only to lift the phone, and they will come and meet you anywhere you say, David"

"Do you trust them, Janet?"

"If the president's involved, yes, David."

Janet called the two agents. They couldn't have been far from the pub, as they turned up five minutes after Janet phoned them. They looked like a couple of Jehovah Witnesses, smartly dressed, not the usual type you would associate with being agents. They were pleasant enough. The taller of the two introduced himself as Fred Bloom and his partner as Eddie Sinclair. "We are glad you agreed to see us, Mr. Martin. I take it Janet has told you why we're here."

"Yes," I said, "but not the real reason why."

"Well, Mr. Martin, the president told us that if you agreed to see him, we were to mention something which would convince you why he had to see you."

I said, "Well, what is the thing you have to tell me?" He seemed to hesitate, then blurted out, "The president said to tell you: 'The list.' "

Janet's head jerked upward in surprise. My own face must have showed some surprise, as he sat there with his know-it-all grin. I asked what he knew about the list.

His face darkened. "Nothing, Mr. Martin. The president just told us to convey that to you if we had this meeting."

"Who else knows about the list apart from you two and the president?"

"We were called into the president's office at the White House." The grin was back on his face.

"Go on," I said.

"There were two of the presidential aides there. The president told us that what we were being asked to do was of national importance and was not to be spoken about after we left the office. He said our department was not to be told what we were doing or where we were destined for."

I stopped him there and asked him if his department was the same one that had been chasing me all over London.

He replied, "Yes, but they had no control over our assignment. They knew nothing of this meeting or the reason for it; even we don't know everything. If you agree to see the president we will fly you from our airbase here in Britain."

I could see Janet was willing to say yes. "Okay, Mr. Bloom, you've got yourself a deal, but I can't go until I've tied some things up here."

His face dropped again. He wouldn't make a good poker player, as he showed too much in his face.

"I'll go with you on Thursday, Mr. Bloom. Contact Janet with where you want to meet me, and she will pass it on to me."

They both stood up and shook my hand.

"Until Thursday then, Mr. Martin," Bloom said. "Good-bye."

"Cheers," I said as Janet and I watched them leave.

I then turned to Janet. "Well, Janet, you haven't told me how you managed to get into the embassy after you left me. Was it you who told them about the farmhouse?"

"Yes, you told me to. I told them everything up to a point. I didn't tell them about the list, and after the president called they took the men who had been following me off. They're not even at my house now."

"Don't trust them too far, Janet; they aren't all like those two who just left."

"Kiss me," she said.

I leaned over and kissed her longingly. The barmaid interrupted by shouting, "I must be good on the phone!" We all laughed.

I was outlining to Janet what I was going to do next when the pub door opened and in walked Gorvik. It was my turn not to have a poker face. He was smiling as if he'd just won the pools. I got up and ushered him to a seat beside me. Janet couldn't believe he was the man who had been taken to St. Mary's a short time ago; neither could I.

Gorvik held both hands up to stop us from asking or saying anything. "I will explain everything," he said. He started to relate how he had got out of hospital and didn't seem to be injured. As soon as he mentioned John and the disciples, I knew what had happened to him was the same thing that had happened to me, but I let him tell it for Janet's sake. If she had any doubts about my story, this would take them away.

Gorvik finished his story and Janet was totally convinced that what he had gone through was true. She said, "I'm sorry for doubting you, David."

"That's okay, love. There will be a lot more doubters before we're finished." I then asked Janet if she had heard anything about the first prediction, as I hadn't seen a paper or any other news media. She said that it happened just as I had said—France had made some incursion against Libya.

I then turned to Gorvik and asked if he had said anything to John about my having to meet Peter about the questions from Sir George Anders. He said he had, just as John was leaving him at the pub door.

Janet asked, "Was he just outside the door, one of the disciples?" She looked like a girl whose favorite pop idol had just arrived. "What did John say about Peter meeting us?"

"Just that he would seek you out in due course."

We then discussed our next move: finding somewhere to stay before any of the agencies found us. I looked at Janet for help in that direction.

She came up with: "Why not a hotel again?"

"We've not got any money left," I said. "Hotels are costly."

We then pooled our resources and had the grand total of ninety pounds.

Janet suggested she could get some more money out of her bank, as she had one of those plastic bank cards. "I think it gives a maximum of two hundred pounds on any one day," she said.

"That will do nicely," I said. "How long will you be?"

"There's one in Oxford Street; give me ten minutes."

While Janet got the money I told Gorvik what I wanted him to do. "Listen, Gorvik, I want you to go to Sir George

50

Anders' house. I'll phone him before you leave." Gorvik was against going, until I told him why it was better all round if he went. "When you get there, tell Sir George your story and what happened after you were shot; this will convince him that my own story may be true. Tell him about tomorrow's predictions and that we have only eight days left for someone to take action to stop the final prediction coming true. I want you to stay there, Gorvik, at least until Friday." I explained to Gorvik where I was going on Thursday.

He asked, "Do you trust them?"

"I don't have much option," I replied. "They don't come any higher than the president of the United States, and if I can convince him that I'm telling the truth or make him think about it we're halfway to winning."

Gorvik nodded his approval at this.

Janet came back with the money. I explained our next moves to her.

She asked, "What about you, David?"

"Well, my original plan for getting Gorvik out of the hospital no longer matters, so I'm going to stay at the Mount Pleasant Hotel until Thursday. When the time comes you can tell your friends to pick me up there for our journey to America. Gorvik can tell Sir George what the predictions will be up until Friday; by that time I should be back in England."

I then called Sir George. Luckily enough, he was at home and not at one of his many clubs. He wasn't too pleased at what I told him but would go along with the idea. He asked if I got any reply to his two questions yet. I told him I would have some answer before Thursday and put the phone down. I hoped I would have some answers for him. Peter had better turn up before Thursday. I told Janet where the car was parked and asked if she would go and get it and come back for me. I gave Gorvik thirty pounds and told him Sir George's address. He would have to get a taxi and take it right to Sir George's front door, I didn't want the security agents to get to Gorvik before Sir George. I said good-bye to Gorvik. He said, "Good luck, David," and went out the pub door.

A couple of minutes later Janet appeared. "Where's Gorvik?"

"He's gone to Sir George's. Let's go," I said.

The barmaid shouted, "Cheerio, lovers!" as we left. Janet smiled. The Mount Pleasant Hotel was on a quiet street with very little traffic except for taxis stopping to let people off at the hotel itself. Janet came up to my room and stayed for an hour. Before she left she said she would phone me every day from a call box, as coming here would be too dangerous after tonight.

FOUR

Harry Black was sitting at his desk inside the American embassy. Chester Manns was wearing the thick-piled carpet down walking back and forth. "Sit down, Chess!" Harry shouted. "Let's try and work out what's going on by putting together what we know." Chester sat down. "Right. First of all, our boss back in the States won't tell us what the hell this Martin guy knows and what we're supposed to find out from him; secondly, we've been told to lay off this Janet dame, who is our only lead so far in finding Martin."

Chess interrupted, "Do you think anything Martin told us was true when we had him at the safe house? You know, about the disciples and the rest of it?"

"Come on, Chess, that's just a lot of rubbish, miracles and disciples helping him to escape from hospital. That's some sort of loony cover story thought up by their inept security."

"Why were we ordered to eliminate Martin, the bombing of the pub? That was a mistake. Then the fiasco outside the hospital—if the British ever find out we did that they'll throw the book at us. Then the boss tells us not to kill him and find out what he knows instead."

"Well, Chess, when the boss calls maybe he'll give us some of the answers. I've left a message with his secretary to call me as soon as he comes in. Meanwhile we will put the guys back on the house of the secretary, get her tailed wherever she goes. After all, it wasn't our boss who called us off it. Won't do any harm if the guys keep a low profile. Go and make arrangements, Chess. I'll give you a buzz when the boss has called and let you know the score."

"I hope you're right, Harry. Our necks could be on the line."

"Don't worry, Chess. The boss and us are in too deep for him to drop the two of us in the shit. If he hasn't told them at the top what's going on, that's his worry; we only follow orders."

After Chess had left, Harry thought to himself the quicker they got stateside, the safer he would feel; this little lot was beginning to smell.

Two hours later Harry was still at his desk. He had put a call out for Chess to return to the embassy. The phone call he had received from his boss in the States had shaken him.

Chess came in slightly out of breath. "Have you heard about the shooting, Harry?"

"No! What's been going on?"

"One of our agents has been shot dead," Chess said.

"How did it happen?"

"He was staking out the safe house when he thought he saw David Martin approaching the place. The idiot got out of the car with the gun in his hand, the other fellow pulled his gun, and both fired at the same time. Our man was killed. The other guy was just wounded. He was taken to hospital but has since disappeared.

"Our man was dragged into his car by his mate and taken to one of the safe houses. No one knows we were involved; it's all been taken care of."

"Thank God for that," Harry said. "We've lost two men today. Someone's going to start asking questions back home and the boss doesn't want that to happen just yet."

"What did you put the call out for me for, Harry?"

"The boss called me from Washington. I told him what has happened so far and that we had been ordered to leave off Martin and Janet. He blew his top; he knew nothing about the order. He asked me where the order came from. I told him the White House. That seemed to be a bigger shock to him than the order to stop operations. I thought he had hung up on me, but he hadn't. I then asked him for information on why we were after Martin. What he told me was along the same lines as the rubbish Martin told us. He said it was a religious cult set on destroying the economy of the United States. The Russians are involved somewhere along the way. But the worst thing he said was the White House knows nothing about this operation and it's to stay that way until further orders tell us different. When I protested at this he said we were too far involved to change course now. In other words, Chess, if this goes wrong, me and you are in shit street. The boss also told me to find out at all costs what Janet knows about this and relay the information to him as soon as possible."

"I don't like this," Chess said. "She's one of our own people, and falling for a Limey isn't a crime. She's helped Martin, but that's no reason for us to treat her like an enemy."

"Listen, Chess, if what the boss has told me is true we've got to do as he says; we're too deep in this thing to change course now."

"Okay, Harry, if you say so, but I don't like it."

"Pick her up when she leaves for work in the morning, and don't balls it up, Chess, take her to one of the safe houses. Let me know in the morning. I want you to question her yourself. Take one man with you, someone who can be trusted; the less people know the better. Now get some sleep; you'll be up early tomorrow."

"Right, Harry. See you in the morning, good night."

Harry sat there till well after midnight. His thoughts weren't very pleasant. The boss seemed to be keeping something back from him, and the fact that he was doing it without telling his own superiors in the White House bothered Harry.

The boss was a lawyer before he entered the agency, but he dealt with the financial side of the law and not the criminal side. They say he would have had his own law business if he hadn't left his job to work for the government. He was working for the agency before the present White House staff appeared on the scene. He had met the president and been photographed shaking his hand. It hung on the wall at the agency, a small brass plate proclaiming his name: CLARENCE FOSTER AND THE PRESIDENT. (With a name like Clarence no wonder he told everybody to call him "Boss.") After Watergate all clandestine operations were to be sanctioned through the phone and his instructions after Harry told him the White House had called off their tail on Martin and the girl was one of fear. *He was hiding something from me. After we get this girl to talk I'm going stateside to see Foster, whether he likes it or not,* Harry decided.

FIVE

Gorvik took the taxi right up to Sir George's door. As he made his way out of the taxi, two men were approaching from the wooded side of the house, but before they reached the taxi Sir George opened the door and shook hands with Gorvik while waving to the two agents that everything was okay. Sir George ushered Gorvik into the main hall and along to his study. Sir George closed the door and invited Gorvik to sit down.

"What will you have to drink, Mr. Gorvik, vodka?"

"No, whiskey, Sir George."

Sir George looked pleased. "I thought all you Russians drank vodka."

"Only in films and comic books, Sir George."

"Well, Mr. Gorvik, David wants me to keep you here until Friday. He said you would have some information and your side of the story to tell me."

"That's correct, Sir George. As it's one o'clock on Tuesday morning I'd better tell you the second prediction before it gets much later and relate my own story afterwards. This prediction will take place at precisely 4 P.M. today, Tuesday, the eighth of June. At that time Iraq will surrender to Iran, due to overwhelming forces of manpower and weapons. The surrender will be unconditional."

Sir George stood at the log fire, his mouth slightly agape. "That's impossible. Their offensive hasn't started yet; our intelligence reports said they were still building their forces up for a final assault against Iraq. If you're correct their attack

57

must have started now. I'm sorry, Gorvik; help yourself to another drink while I make a phone call."

Sir George left the room. He went to the front door and called the two MI6 agents over; he then proceeded with them in tow towards their own private room. Once there he told one of them to call his chief.

It was Wells who spoke first. "We can't just call the head of our department at one-thirty in the morning unless it's urgent."

"It's urgent alright," Sir George replied, "so call him. I'll take full responsibility." Wells called his superior. The phone was answered almost immediately.

"Hello, sir, Louis Wells here. . . . Yes, sir. I'm one of the agents at Sir George Anders' residence." Louis looked relieved that his boss was taking it so calmly with it being so late. "He would like to speak to you, sir."

"Put him on, Louis.

"Hello, Tom, sorry if I have disturbed your sleep."

"That's okay, Sir George, goes with the job. What do you want?"

"Well, Tom, have you heard anything in your section about the Middle East?"

"What part of the Middle East are you talking about, George?"

"Iran or Iraq, Tom?"

"Nothing has been passed on to me on any new developments in that area, Sir George. Is there something I should know about?"

"Could you check something for me, Tom? Find out if Iran has made any fresh moves against Iraq?"

"I can find out first thing in the morning, George, and let you know."

"That's no good, Tom. I want that information now, if there is any."

"Can you tell me what's supposed to be happening that's so important and will mean me having to go to Whitehall at two o'clock in the morning?"

"I'm sorry, Tom."

"If my information is correct, you will be coming with me to see the prime minister later this morning. You think your information is that important?"

"Yes, Tom, I do."

"Okay, Sir George, I'll get back to you if there's anything important on what you ask. Put Louis back on, will you?"

"Right, Tom, good-bye."

"Cheerio, George."

Sir George handed the phone back to Louis Wells and returned to Gorvik. "Well, Mr. Gorvik, if you'll follow me I'll take you to your room and you can tell me your story there."

Louis Wells was listening to his boss asking if Sir George had been out last night and where he had been. Louis told him that he hadn't been out, but he had a visitor who was still here and looked as if he was staying.

"Who is he? Do you know him?"

"No, I've never seen him before, sir."

"I'll be calling back later on, so stay awake."

"Right, sir, good-bye."

After Janet left, I showered and called room service for a sandwich and coffee. I was sitting thinking of all that had taken place so far when I felt this presence behind me. I turned my head; it was Peter. "I'm glad to see you, Peter," I said.

"You're looking good, David. You seem to be taking the strain well."

"Seeing you has helped, Peter. Gorvik told John I wanted to see you?"

"Yes, he told me, David. Now what is that you want? Before you tell me, David, I'd better tell you this will be the last time

59

we meet or that I will be able to help you until the last day of the predictions; that will be on the sixteenth of June. Now tell me what you want, David."

"First, Peter, why is this the last time you can help me? What if things start to go wrong? Whom do I go to for help?"

"I'm sorry, David, but you will have to make do with the knowledge and people who are involved at this stage. We can no longer become known to any more people. As we said at the start, that could have as bad an effect as the thing we're trying to stop. The people so far involved either do not believe we are who we say we are or they are doubtful. We would like to keep it that way and hope that those in power believe you through what has already happened. The predictions will help you more than we can now."

"Okay, Peter, I have certain questions to ask you. They come from my own boss, Sir George Anders. He said if these questions were given answers that could be substantiated he would believe my story and that the final prediction will come true. He will do everything he can to convince the prime minister that it will happen as I have said it would."

"Right, David. Give me your questions."

"There are two, Peter. The first is: Is Charles Darwin's theory on evolution, of man coming from apes, true? The second question is: Why did the dinosaurs all disappear at the same time and for what reason?" I was kind of curious what the answers would be myself.

"Well, David, both these questions had answers put to them by men. They have come close to the correct answers in their search for the truth of how it all began. In Darwin's case, his theory of man coming from apes, the truth of that is the reverse—the apes were created by man." I sat there spellbound. I was hearing what every scientist would give his right arm to hear. "You will know, David, either through reading or being told by people who have witnessed it, that mankind has for millions of years cavorted with animals; this was how apes came from man and not the other way around."

I had heard these stories about people in certain remote areas having sex with animals of various types. This was true of both sexes and still happened to the present day. I only hoped it was enough for Sir George to convince him.

Peter continued, "The answer to the second question is far more complicated, but I will try to explain it so that it becomes easy to understand. Man was around when dinosaurs were here. The reason for their extinction was a new ice age. Your scientists were correct in their assumption that this was the main cause of their downfall. It came about by volcanic eruptions.

"You have to remember that the earth was still relatively young and eruptions were still an everyday occurrence, but there came a time when the eruptions coincided with each other. If you can imagine five hundred mountains erupting at the same time it will give you some idea of the effect it had on this planet. For ten months the sun was virtually blotted out. This created a new ice age that killed off nearly every big animal that couldn't survive without the heat of the sun, and the foliage which sustained them was virtually killed off."

"But how did man survive all that, Peter?"

"This is the hard part to try and explain, David. While all the dinosaurs died, or most of them, man was very resourceful even then. He was different in appearance than he is today. God made it that way just for this eventuality. Mankind and the dinosaurs could no longer live together; man would not survive if they were allowed to survive.

"The dinosaurs had served their purpose; that was to fertilize the earth. That was the reason they were given their great size. I will not go into too much detail on this; it would take too long. But man survived through various means on all continents. You have to remember the continents were closer

61

together and not separated as they are today. As the ice age progressed many died, but more survived. The best example I can give you is what is known today as the Tibetan yeti."

I looked at Peter in amazement. "Then the stories of the yeti are true," I said.

"Yes, David, they are. Some of man's past relations have survived till the present day. One shall be found in the near future, and man shall revise his history of many things, including Darwin's theory of the evolution of man. Well, David, I hope that will help convince Sir George."

"Well, Peter, I've got some things that I would like answers to."

"Yes, I know, David, but your time for answers has not arrived. You will be able to ask your questions after this task has been finalized."

"Okay, Peter. I'll not see you again until this is all over? I'll not be able to call on you for any more help if I get into difficulty?"

"That's correct, David, but I'm sure you will manage somehow." At that Peter shook my hand and wished me luck, then left.

Seconds after the door closed I thought I would look out and see what way he went, but as usual when I looked along a hotel corridor there was no one in sight. I wished I could disappear so quickly; it would be helpful in escaping from people I didn't want to meet.

I had two days to kill before my journey to the States. I looked at my watch—it was 4 A.M., Gorvik would have told Sir George about today's prediction. I wondered what his reaction was. I would phone Sir George in the morning and get his reaction myself.

Sir George got his answer from Tom McAlister two hours after he called him. He and Gorvik had talked for some time on Gorvik's story and Russia. When Tom phoned he was very upset; he wanted to know the full details of how Sir George had got information that his security people hadn't even had a whiff of. Iran had made a big push on all fronts and was having great success in the first couple of hours of their offensive. Sir George told Tom to meet him at ten in the morning. They would both be having a meeting with the prime minister, and answers to her questions would have to be given.

Sir George had a couple of hours' sleep. He was having his breakfast before meeting Tom McAlister when the phone rang. It was David Martin.

"Hello, David. What's new this morning?"

"Sir, I've got a reply on your two questions from last week."

"That's good, David. Can you tell me over the phone, or will I come and see you later?"

"No, Sir George, I don't think that's a good idea. You know the reasons why not. What I'll do, sir, is write the answers to your questions and send them to you. They're a bit long-winded to convey over the phone, and we don't know who's listening, do we?"

This made Sir George laugh. He had an idea his phones were tapped, too. I asked Sir George about a certain prediction for today and was there any news?

"Yes, David, that information was confirmed last night, or should I say early this morning."

"That's good, Sir George. Well, I won't keep you any longer, sir."

"Keep in touch, David, good-bye."

Sir George was still smiling when he sat back down to his breakfast. He knew that the security men would be pretty mad, as they wanted David as badly as the Americans wanted him. That's why he had used David's name over the phone. They

63

wouldn't question him on it, as that would confirm their phone tap on his private phone. His smile broadened.

Janet felt good when she woke this morning. Knowing David was pretty safe and that he would be meeting the president of the United States made her feel better than she had for days. The president's call to the embassy seemed to have taken the pressure off her worrying about her security people. While she was dressing, a car pulled up at the curb of the street outside her flat. Inside were Chester Manns and a newcomer to the embassy security service, Joe Simms. Joe was pretty nervous. He had been in the service for two years. Landing a job in the American embassy in Britain was unusual with only two years' service. They generally used older hands for these posts. As an ex-soldier, he was more used to giving advice to people on what arms or tactics to use, as he had done in Nicaragua for the contras. He had requested a transfer, as he thought his job in Nicaragua was a waste of time. He didn't tell his superiors that, of course, just that he wanted to be transferred. Chess had told him they had a job to do in the morning and it involved the embassy secretary. He said she was under suspicion of having given information to a foreign power and they were to question her until they got some answers. Joe had collected the keys to one of the safe houses on his way to the car. He wanted to make a good impression on Chester, as he was second in command to Mr. Black and if Joe made good on this assignment he believed he would be kept at the embassy instead of being given some mundane job outside of it.

Janet had decided to leave a couple of minutes early. She wanted to phone David and the phone in her flat might be bugged, so she would call from the phone box across the road. Chess nudged Joe in the side as Janet's door opened. She came down the steps and walked straight across the road to the phone box.

"Turn the car around, Joe. We'll pick her up at the phone box," Chess said.

Janet had just got through to David when the phone box door opened and this man told her she was needed at the embassy right away.

Janet told David to hold for a minute while she spoke to someone. She recognized the man's face from the embassy but couldn't remember his name, as he was new to the embassy. She asked him what was so important it couldn't wait for two minutes. It was then she stooped down to see who was in the car. As soon as she saw who it was, she dropped the phone and shoved the man who had asked her to come to the embassy. He fell against the car, and she ran up the road. Before she got fifty yards the car had pulled up beside her and the man she had shoved jumped out and grabbed her arm. She struggled with him, then heard Chester Manns shout, "Hit her and get her in the car!" Joe didn't like doing it, but the blow to Janet's chin didn't know that. She went out like a light. Chess left the engine running and gave Joe a hand to get her in the backseat of the car. The whole episode had taken two minutes to complete. The car sped off to the safe house.

David was worried. Janet had only been on the phone a few seconds. He had heard Janet speaking to someone; then there was nothing. The phone must have been left off the hook, as there was no dial tone. It hurt to think she might be in danger and he could do nothing about it. He didn't know where she had phoned from. It wasn't her flat—the bleeps had told him that. He felt useless. He sat down and tried to think what action he could take to help her. He thought of calling the American embassy and trying to speak to the two agents who were taking him to America, but there were too many ears there and they may not even be staying there.

It was more likely the person or people who had got Janet were her own agents from the embassy. The president's call might be ignored by them, or they were getting desperate. An idea started to formulate in my head. If it was them, I knew some of them—Mr. H. and Chester Manns. If I could get hold of one of them and make him talk . . . I thought of calling Sir George and getting Gorvik to help me, but he was more valuable where he was. If anything happened to me, Gorvik would be able to carry on with Sir George's help.

I thought of John and Frank, my two workmates. One of them would be enough. Of the two, John was the more reliable one. They would be at the Foreign Office just now. I dialed the number and got the office telephonist to put me through to Sir George's office.

It was Frank who answered the phone. "Good God, is that you, David?"

"Yes, Frank."

He wanted to know everything that I had been doing. He said Sir George had told him all enquiries were to be passed to him. I interrupted Frank and asked him to put John on the line, as I hadn't much time.

John must have been standing right next to Frank, as he replied almost immediately, "Yes, David?"

"Look, John, I need your help, but it can't be known that you're doing so, not even Frank and especially not Sir George." I arranged to meet John at one of our old haunts. He said they were busy, but he would give Frank some cock-and-bull story so he would cover for him. John would meet me at twelve o'clock at the wine bar on Duke Street. Before I hung up I told John to make sure he took precautions.

I got ready right away, checking the gun that I had taken from the dead agent at the farm. It was loaded, I hoped it wouldn't be needed, but I wanted to check the American embassy before meeting John so I could work out how to go about getting our man. The car was a must if we were to succeed.

I got to the embassy about ten-thirty. Plenty of time to work out our tactics. I wouldn't be able to drive near the embassy, as it was cordoned off with barrier rails. This was done after the Barred bombing by suicide drivers with trucks full of explosives. They were afraid it could happen here, hence the barriers.

John was at the wine bar exactly on time. I had been there about half an hour. I had worked out our plan of action. I told John what I wanted him to do. He was to stay with the car until I signalled from my vantage point facing the embassy. The car was parked as near as possible to our target, on a street to the left of the front entrance. It had double yellows, but we would have to take a chance on not being clamped or towed away. It would be alright once John was sitting in it; he could move if need be.

When he saw me signal him he was to start the engine and get ready to collect me. We would then, if possible, bundle our target into the car if he was walking. If, on the other hand, he was using a car we would follow him. John was looking forward to it all. This was better than the movies, he said. I told him not to be too sure; there had been a few bodies left around on this caper as it was. He was a bit more subdued, but the twinkle was still in his eyes. "Right, let's move, John," I told him.

I showed John where the car was and pointed to where I would be standing. He said he would see me okay.

It was chilly after one hour of watching the front entrance. There were plenty of people coming and going, but no one I recognized. I hoped John wouldn't be asleep in the car just when I needed him. It was three o'clock and I was beginning to tire of standing and also needed the toilet. I started to go towards the car when Harry Black came out of the front entrance. I stopped and watched where he was making for. He was heading towards the shopping precinct; there were numerous sandwich bars and cafes there. I only hoped he was going to one.

I turned to John and signalled for him to go round the embassy to the other side. I pointed to a corner where he could park. Meanwhile Harry had gone into one of the cafes. I crossed the road and waited for John to appear with the car. While keeping an eye on the cafe I could see John turning into the street. He pulled up to the curb.

"The man we want is in the restaurant; keep the engine running and stand with me. When he comes out, open the back door; I'll force him inside. If things go wrong, get into the car and drive off, with or without me."

"I know I haven't asked, David, but why do you want to question this man?"

"Okay, John, I'll tell you, but remember: don't tell anyone what we've been doing or why. I think this man has kidnapped Janet."

"What! But why, David? She bloody well works there."

"It's a long story, John, too long to go into just now; you'll just have to take my word for it. This man or someone under his control I believe has Janet."

The twinkle had gone from John's eyes. In its place was a determined look of revenge. He knew Janet as well as I did and liked her just as much.

I turned my back and faced John. Harry had just come out of the cafe. "Here he comes, John. Get ready." I timed my turning till Harry was near enough for me to stick the gun in his ribs. The shock in his face was enough to make me realize we would have no struggle from him. "Get in the back, Harry," I said.

John shoved him into the seat, then ran to the driver's side. I got in beside Harry.

"Where to, David?" John asked.

"Take the motorway out of London. I'll give you directions from there."

I was going to the farmhouse on the Holmoor Road. I couldn't think of anywhere else to go that was safe enough to question someone. When we hit the motorway I told John to turn off when he came to it. I turned to Harry and asked him bluntly where Janet was.

"How the hell should I know, Martin? You had better turn this thing around and get me back to the embassy before I'm missed."

"I don't like your tone, Harry. I want answers and I want them quickly."

"Piss off, Limey!"

I cracked him with the gun across the face. Blood spurted from his nose.

"You bastard!" he said.

"What's wrong, Harry? Can't take it as well as you dish it out?"

He pulled a handerchief from his pocket and held it to his nose. While he did that I frisked him for any weapons; he had none.

I told John to take the next turning on the left. Ten minutes later we were on the Holmoor Road. "Pull in here, John." We were fifty yards from the farm. "I'll check if it's clear, John. Take this gun. If he moves, shoot him."

"It'll be a pleasure, David. I hope he does." John looked as if he meant it, too.

I walked right up to the farmhouse door. It looked deserted, but I had thought that the last time and I was wrong. I knocked on the door. If anyone came I would pretend to have trouble with my car. But there was no reply to my knocking and the door had been secured with a new lock. I gave it a push. It wasn't that secure, so I put my full weight against it, and it gave.

I checked the inside. There were no signs of anything having happened here. I could still see in my mind the two agents lying on the floor. The Americans had made a good job of cleaning up the evidence of anything ever having happened here. I went outside and waved John to drive up. He drove with one hand on the wheel and the other covering Harry with the gun.

"Park the car up the back of the farmhouse, John."

"Right. Harry, get out of the car."

I took Harry inside, the gun in his back. "Sit down," I said, "and don't try anything stupid, Harry."

John came in and closed the door.

"There should be an old oil lamp lying about, John. See if you can find it before it gets dark."

John got the lamp going while I tied up Harry to an old chair with some old rags.

"What happens now, David?" John asked.

"We make this bastard talk; that's what happens next. You're going to talk, Harry, and they better be the right answers you give."

"I told you before, Martin, fuck off."

"Bring the lamp over, John."

He put the lamp on the table next to me. There was some loose straw in one of the corners. I took some strands and lit one. "Hold his hand out, John."

John hesitated but did as he was told.

"You can go outside if you want, John. I'll do it myself if you want."

"No, it's okay, David. Do what you have to do."

I held the lit straw under Harry's hand. Harry let out a scream; at the same time, the chair he was tied to toppled over backwards. His head hit the stone floor with a crack. John and

I lifted the chair back up, but Harry was out cold. Sweat was running down John's face, I knew he didn't like this, neither did I, but these people didn't understand any other way.

John asked what we were going to do if and when we got Harry to talk. I told him we could leave him tied up and then phone the embassy as to where he was.

"Are you going to do any more of this burning of the hands bit, David?"

"I'll do what's necessary to make him talk, John. I don't like this any more than you do, but these bastards have done me over and as far as I know killed a few people into the bargain, so if I have to chop his bloody hands off to make him talk, I will."

"Okay, David, you've been put through the mill with these people and know more of what's going on than I do, so count me in to the finish."

"Thanks, John. Get me some water from the kitchen. I'll throw some over him."

Harry spluttered as the water hit him. His eyes were still glazed, and his face grimaced in pain.

"Right. Harry, do we talk now or go through it all over again?" Before he answered, I asked John to get me some more straw.

Harry yelled, "No! I'll tell you what I know!"

I looked at John. I could see the relief on his face. "Okay, Harry, let's hear what you know."

He started by telling me if he lived he was going to kill me.

I replied, "You tried before and if you try again I promise you that I won't let you off so lightly. Now talk."

He told us where Janet had been taken: "A safe house off Oxford Street. I think it's called Duke Street."

"I know where it is," I replied. "Your safe houses seem too

close together. That one's just two streets away from the one on James Street."

"That's right, Martin. When you get there I hope they blow your head off."

"How many will be with Janet, Harry?"

"How the fuck should I know? I've been here with you."

Harry gave us the number of the house. I told him if his information was wrong, I would come back and personally break his neck, and if he was telling the truth, we would get someone here to free him.

I checked his arms and legs were secure before we left. He said something as we went, but the swelling of the nose and mouth made it unintelligible. I told John to head for Oxford Street. While driving to London John made the observation that I had changed, become more hard. I told him if I hadn't I would have been dead.

John then asked me how serious it was between Janet and me. I replied, "I'm going to marry her the first chance I get." Saying it and thinking it were two different things. It was a shock to hear myself say I would marry Janet. The small ache in my chest wasn't there through injury, it was for Janet. I just hadn't admitted it to myself up until now.

"What's our next move, David, if we manage to get Janet back?"

"I'll have to think about that, John."

SIX

Chess and Joe got to the safe house ten minutes after they lifted Janet. The main street in front of the house was busy with people. Chess suggested to Joe that he lift Janet in his arms as if they were frolicking. "Swing her round and pretend you're laughing; then get into the doorway of the house. I'll open the door first; then make your move."

Joe got out of the car. He opened the door and pulled Janet towards him. She was quite light. He lifted her with ease. Joe started laughing and twirling with Janet towards the door of the safe house. People who did pass them simply smiled. Chess ushered him into the house and said, "You'll likely get an Oscar for that." Joe didn't answer him; he was thinking how warm the girl's body was in his arms. She was really beautiful; he felt sorry that he had to hit her.

Chess interrupted his thoughts by telling him to take her to the bedroom while he phoned Harry. Chess got through to Harry right away. Harry asked how it had gone.

"It went like clockwork, Harry. How far have we to go to make her talk?"

"Do what you have to, but get her to talk. You know we can't let her go even if she does talk, so once you're finished with her get rid of Simms, back to the embassy, then take care of the girl."

Chess didn't like that part and said so to Harry.

"What do you want to do, Chess? Let her go to tell everything she knows?"

"You're right, Harry. I'll call you when I've got something

from her. When Simms comes to the embassy you better have a word with him about keeping his mouth shut."

"You take care of the girl; I'll look after Simms." At that Harry hung up.

Chess returned to Simms and told him to take the car back to the embassy, then go and see Harry when he arrived there.

"What about the girl?" Joe said.

"Just leave her to me; you get back to the embassy."

Joe didn't like leaving, but he hadn't much choice. He looked in on the girl before leaving. She looked very peaceful lying there. He turned to say something to Chess but changed his mind and just left.

Chess closed and bolted the door. He got some rope from one of the hall cupboards, then proceeded to tie both Janet's arms to the brass bedposts. The same was done to her legs, spread apart and tied to the bed. While Chess was doing this the bulge in his trousers was getting bigger. The thought of doing anything he wanted to this beautiful girl got his blood boiling. He thought to himself, *I'm going to have to kill her anyway, so why shouldn't I have some fun before I do? I'll wait until she wakes, get her to tell what she knows, then have my fun.* He then went to have some breakfast in the kitchen. The bad thoughts he had about killing her had diminished somewhat when he thought of what was to come.

Janet woke up and found her arms and legs firmly tied. Her jaw was stiff, and she could hardly open her mouth. She struggled with her bonds, but they were only cutting into her arms and legs the more she tried to move. She looked about her. The room was spacious. She could tell it was still light outside. The curtains were drawn, but light still showed through them. She surmised this was one of their own safe houses, but had no idea where it was or how far from the embassy. She knew they were close to one another. Her thoughts were interrupted by the bedroom door opening.

Chester Manns's head came round the door. When he saw she was awake he came right into the room. "Hello, Janet," he said.

Janet grimaced at him. She felt pretty vulnerable lying here and had never liked Chester Manns even before this happened. He sat on the edge of the bed.

"How's your chin feeling?"

He put his hands on her face as if this would take or ease the pain. She pulled her head away. The slap he gave her was unexpected, and the tears started down her face.

"I don't want to hurt you, Janet; all I want is the whereabouts of David Martin and anything else you know about him."

"You can go to hell, Manns!"

"Okay, Janet, if that's the way you want to play it."

Janet watched him get up and leave the room. Her stomach was turning with fear. The door reopened and Chess came in. Janet noticed he had something in his hand.

"Are you sure you still want to say nothing, Janet?"

She didn't even reply to his question. Chess knelt at the bottom of the bed. Janet could see what he was holding: scissors. He was leering at her. He put his hand on her left leg, then positioned himself in a kneeling pose between her legs. Janet was ready to throw up. Chess got hold of her hemline. The way her legs were positioned made her plain tweed skirt tight against her knees.

Chess started at the center of the skirt and proceeded to cut his way up to her waistline. Before he reached there Janet, trying to keep calm, asked if it wouldn't be easier to untie her and let her undress. Chess looked as if he hadn't even heard her. He cut the skirt to where Janet's panties were showing, Janet didn't have any nylons on. She was used to the sunbed giving her legs the right colour, so that she wore nylons very rarely. Chess's hands were shaking slightly. He stopped to admire his handiwork. His hands started to caress the inside of Janet's thighs. She started to struggle, throwing her hips from side to side. This seemed only to excite Manns more. He placed his hands on Janet's stomach and leaned on her. This stopped Janet's efforts of struggle. She looked pleadingly at Chester, but she knew nothing was going to stop him now. He pulled her skirt from under her, and Janet screamed. Chester slapped her across the face. Again she went quiet. Janet's blouse was the pullover type, no buttons except for three at the top of the neckline. He started to cut away at the blouse in the same manner as he had done with the skirt.

John and I parked the car some distance from the safe house, not because we wanted to, but parking restrictions made it impossible for us to get any closer with the car. It had taken us over an hour to get there; the traffic had built up and hindered our speed.

We found Duke Street to be a busy place; the big department stores were nearby and shoppers were out in force. I suggested to John that we should look for another means of entry, as the front door was very conspicuous to try and kick in. We both walked round the entire building, but there was no other entrance that would allow us easy access.

John said, "It looks like the front is the only way in."

I agreed. "But it's too busy to go charging at the front doors. We don't want the police involved, and they would be called in minutes with this mob going up and down the street."

"What do we do in the meantime?" John asked. "Find ourselves a quiet boozer till the stores close?"

I didn't like the idea of waiting, but there was no other way without attracting attention to ourselves.

I took John to the pub he had gone to after escaping from

the last safe house. John ordered two large lagers, and we picked a quiet corner to sit in. The stores would be starting to close in three-quarters of an hour.

"Well, John, you can still back out before we tackle the safe house. You've done enough already, and Sir George won't like it too much if anything happens to you."

"Forget it, David. I haven't enjoyed myself so much in donkeys' years."

I knew that John was a bit apprehensive about it all but would come through alright.

John asked when I was going to phone the American embassy so they could release Harry Black.

"I'll phone as soon as we get Janet released from their safe house. If I phone too soon they might get here before we're finished rescuing Janet; that's if everything goes alright. We don't know how many are in there, and if it goes wrong we can always bargain with Harry." I gave John a nudge. It was time to go. Duke Street was a lot quieter, the odd person coming and going but nothing compared to what it had been.

"The two of us will hit the door at the same time, John."

We both put our shoulders to the door, leaned back, and hit it at the same time. It gave slightly.

"One more should do it, John."

We both repeated the action. This time the door gave way. We both went in at the same time. I pulled the gun from my jacket. If anyone was here, they would have heard the door go. I told John to stay behind me as I opened the door to the left, I shoved the door wide and crouched down. The room was empty. I turned to John. He had a smile on his face. I knew what he was smiling at, me crouching after opening the door. I felt stupid; I'd seen too many gangster movies.

I pointed to the next door on the right. John tapped my shoulder and pointed to himself. I handed him the gun. John shoved the door wide and stepped inside. I followed quickly at his back. John stopped in his tracks; he turned round, trying to stop me going farther into the room. It was obvious why. There was blood all over the bed to our left. There was no topsheet, just the undersheet visible. My chest had an ache as it was hard to take a breath. John was chalk white. We both moved farther into the room. At the other side of the bed was the topsheet from the bed; it was saturated with blood. One leg was showing from the end of the sheet.

I froze.

John turned and looked at me. "Why don't you wait in the hall, David?"

"No, John, I'll do it."

I stepped round. John pulled the sheet from the body. I could hear John being sick behind me. I was ready to throw up as well. It was Janet—she was dead. I felt like screaming.

I started to shake uncontrollably when I felt John pulling me to my feet.

"Lets get the police, David," John said.

"No!" I shouted.

John looked startled.

"I'm sorry, John, but I'm going to take care of this myself."

"How, David? We don't know who's responsible."

"Maybe not, but I know who can tell us—Harry."

We both stripped the sheet off the bed and laid Janet on top of the bare mattress.

The reason for all the blood became obvious. Her neck had a wound that was right on her jugular vein; the blood would have pumped out of her in minutes. I told John that I was going to kill whoever had done this.

John looked at me and said, "You won't get me slacking if you need a hand to do it."

"First, John, we have to get back to the farmhouse and talk to Harry." I leaned over Janet and kissed her white lips.

John could see the tears in my eyes. Going by the look on my face while we drove to the farmhouse, John didn't give Harry much chance of leaving there alive.

We got to the farmhouse twenty minutes quicker than it took to get from there to the safe house. I rushed up to the farmhouse door; it was open. I went inside, gun at the ready. Harry was gone. The chair was lying on its side; the rags were lying on the floor.

I turned to John. "Let's have a look about outside. He may still be about."

There was no sign of Harry.

"What do we do now?" John asked.

"Head back to London," I replied. "You can contact Sir George, John; I'll drop you off. Tell him what happened and where I'll be staying."

"I'll stick with you if you want, David."

"No, John, the people involved in this are beginning to lose control of their actions through panic. I have to get to this other meeting tomorrow. Janet would have wanted me to do this. I'll take care of Harry and his pals as soon as I've completed this mission."

I dropped John off. We both wished each other luck; then I drove to the hotel. I stopped worrying about who might see me or if Janet had told them anything before she died. Just thinking of Janet made me feel sick and impotent that I couldn't avenge her death. They say men don't show tears, but my eyes were red for the rest of the night.

Sir George had received Martin's answers to his two questions by letter. They were as unreal as the answers about what was going on with disciples and the return of the Messiah. But Sir George had been given another prediction by Gorvik on Wednesday. He predicted that after Iraq fell to the Iranians they were going to put an ultimatum to Saudi Arabia that if they did not help in the coming war with Israel, Iran would attack Arabian military installations. The terms would be given to the Saudis at one o'clock today, Wednesday.

This time it was confirmed by the intelligence service and was true. Sir George hadn't told them how he got the information on the Iran attack and subsequent defeat by the Iranians. The prime minister agreed they should be told, but the time was not right for that. Sir George had smiled inwardly and told the prime minister that he would have more information to relate to her shortly. This he told her after McAlister had left, of course.

She told Sir George to inform her as soon as he had any more information. Sir George had done this with Gorvik's information about Iran and the Saudis. The prime minister was shocked by the information, as the consequences of this action by Iran could affect the world oil supply and create another world slump, from which the world might not be able to recover. She told Sir George that America could be drawn into this conflict if the Iranians carried their threat through.

"We would also have to take action, as the Saudis are great friends of Britain and their trade with us would be sorely missed," she added. "But the main concern will be the oil, as another world recession on top of the last one would destroy a great many democracies. Even we might not survive this one without social unrest." She explained a lot more to Sir George, and he had never seen her as upset as this since coming to the office.

Later that night at Sir George's mansion John arrived to relate what had taken place with David and himself earlier on in the day. Sir George was shaken when he heard about Janet being killed. He asked if John knew who had done it. John told him whom they suspected and what David was going to do when he found them, but he was going to carry out this mission for the disciples and Janet first. Gorvik was told to come down and enter the discussion with them on the question of disciples and Janet's murder.

Sir George put it to Gorvik that if the "disciples" were who they said they were, Janet would still be alive. Gorvik's answer was simple: "There are more people than Janet dying in the world, and this includes young babies by the thousands? Why should one girl be treated differently?"

John said, "But if David's helping the disciples, they would surely help someone who was helping him."

"I don't have the answer to that, but if you ask me if they *are* the disciples, I would have to say yes."

The discussion went on for some hours, with Sir George and John not totally convinced of Gorvik's reasons for being so sure in his convictions.

The discussion had run its course when Gorvik told Sir George that it was time for a further prediction for tomorrow, which was why Gorvik was here. John was as excited as Sir George about what was next on Gorvik's list, which he had hidden after reading what was the next prediction. Gorvik himself didn't believe what he had read, and he had prior knowledge of it.

Gorvik started, "Well, Sir George, this part of the prediction should convince you of the reality of the disciples. Tomorrow at four o'clock, your time, the leader of my country will be killed."

Sir George jumped to his feet. "You mean, Gorvik, that your premier will be assassinated?"

"Yes, Sir George." Gorvik sounded sad.

John looked at Sir George and asked what he thought would happen if this was true. Sir George told him quickly that on top of everything else that was taking place, a change of leadership in the Kremlin, especially with a hardliner taking over at this time, could spell disaster. Sir George excused himself and left the two men looking at each other.

Sir George didn't even worry if the security heard him or not; his phone call was put through to the prime minister right away, even though it was twelve-thirty on Thursday morning. He told the prime minister what Gorvik had said. She ordered him to come down to 10 Downing Street as soon as he was ready. Sir George returned to John and Gorvik and asked John if he could drop him off on the way to the prime minister's. John said yes.

"You'll be okay till I get back, Gorvik?"

"Yes, Sir George, don't worry about me."

Sir George changed his dinner jacket for more suitable attire; then he left with John in tow.

SEVEN

Chester Manns left the safe house; he hadn't even cleaned the place of the evidence of what had happened. He was still quite dazed at what had happened. His orders were to kill Janet when he had the information he needed from her, but the way she died shocked even him. It had been a pure accident, not the way he had planned to kill her. When he was cutting her blouse open he had moved his position over Janet so that his legs were at each side of Janet's waist. That was his mistake. Janet couldn't move any of her limbs, but her hips could move up or sideways. While he was concentrating on her blouse, Janet moved her right hipbone upwards with all her power. She caught Chess between the legs. The force took Chess by complete surprise. He fell off the bed to his right, then sprang to his feet with anger, swinging his right hand as if to slap Janet for what she had done. Chess realized a split second before the blow struck Janet that the scissors were still in his hand.

They pierced Janet's neck right in her jugular vein. The blood was flowing from Janet's neck. Chess tried to stem it with the topsheet of the bed, but it was hopeless. Janet stared at Chess; she knew by looking at him that the wound was serious. She didn't feel much pain after the scissors were withdrawn. In fact, she felt very relaxed and sleepy. She wanted to tell Chess to get David to join her, as she loved him, but no sound came from her lips. Chess sat on the bed holding her hands. He had loosened her bonds. All thought of what he was there for gone, he felt cheap and dirty. She gently passed away like some child going to sleep. Chess lifted her from the bed onto the floor and wrapped the sheet round her. He was covered in her blood. Still dazed, he cleaned himself up and left the safe house with only one thought in his head: to see Harry Black and get himself put stateside right away.

Sir George Anders dropped John off at his home, then proceeded to 10 Downing Street. The policeman on duty knocked on the door for Sir George. He entered and was greeted by the prime minister's secretary. "This way, sir." He took Sir George to one of the conference rooms, of which there were a few in Number 10. Sir George expected to be met by the prime minister and McAlister, but the conference room was full of her close cabinet colleagues, most of whom he knew through past meetings. The prime minister was seated at the head of the table with four ministers on either side of her. McAlister was seated at the far end of the table. He looked a lonely figure sitting there, so Sir George decided to sit next to him. As he sat down the prime minister requested that he tell her ministers what he had told her over the phone.

When Sir George had finished they were as astounded at this information as he had been. The prime minister then asked if he would tell the cabinet the whole story so far. Sir George told the story of David Martin's exploits so far and of Gorvik's involvement in the affair. When he had finished there were questions coming from nearly all the cabinet members. The prime minister stepped in to bring order to the questions being asked. She told the cabinet members that one question she had asked Sir George before, but his answer at that time was negative to it. She repeated, "I shall ask him again if he believes that what Mr. Martin has told him and Mr. Gorvik has changed his view of the truth of these disciples." Sir George looked round the table. Whatever he said would make him look either stupid or insane, but an answer he had to give.

"I am not one hundred percent sure of what these disciples are. If they are just ordinary people, then they are the most organised intelligence network I've heard of. They might be making these events happen through some network of theirs that I can't hope to explain to you, but taking other things which have happened into account, if I and others with whom I work have not been duped, they cannot be easily explained away. The first instance is David Martin's injury disappearing in the hospital not once, but twice. This I would believe would give credence to the truth of David's allegations that these men are from God."

This brought another barrage of questions from the ministers. The prime minister put her hand up for silence. Sir George smiled at the obedience she instilled in grown men in places of power.

"I don't think Sir George can enlighten us any more than he has, gentlemen. We shall just have to wait and see if what he has told us comes true tomorrow. It would be foolish of us to try and warn anyone of this, as we do not know if it will happen. Further, I don't want anyone to speak of this meeting or any of the subjects that were brought up." With this the prime minister closed the meeting. "You, Sir George, and McAlister will stay behind for a short time. I have something to discuss with you both."

When the others had left, the prime minister took both of them into the living room of Number 10. She ordered tea and some sandwiches to be brought.

"Well, Mr. McAlister, what do you think of Sir George's theory of these disciples being an intelligence group?"

McAlister looked at Sir George, then replied that it made more sense than thinking that these people were from God. "I myself don't believe they're an intelligence group. To organize these events they would have to be spread over every country in the world, with access to the very top people in these countries. Our own intelligence network would have been breached, as the others must have been, for them to be able to predict events that have not happened yet. I don't know any network which could pull something like this off, not even the Russians, and theirs is one of the best in the world."

"Thank you, Tom," she said. "You can go home and get some sleep. Report to me just before this next event happens, let's say three-thirty."

After Tom McAlister left, the prime minister asked Sir George if he had any other theory on the subject. Sir George told the prime minister, after some seconds of thought, that after what he had witnessed and after talking to Gorvik, whom he believed to be totally honest and not in anyway involved in a conspiracy to make anyone else look stupid with this story, he believed that these people who controlled David Martin and Gorvik were not of this world. The prime minister asked if he meant they were some sort of spacemen from another planet.

"No, ma'am, that's not what I mean. I believe, and it's the only explanation that fits what happened, that they are the original disciples of Jesus."

"Do you know what this would mean, Sir George, if it's true? And I'm keeping an open mind on this. This would explain why some intelligence groups, either legitimate ones or rogue ones, are trying to kill off anyone involved in this. That would include you as well, Sir George."

Sir George produced the letter he had received in answer to the questions that David had been given. He explained to the prime minister that he had called up a certain professor of Oxford College and asked him if he were to be confronted with someone who said he could tell about the distant past, what he would say to this person to prove that the person was from the distant past. "I also told him that the questions would have to be about religion. The questions and answers are in the letter, Prime Minister."

She read the letter. Sir George was interested to see if the answers made any impression on the prime minister. She looked up after the last page was read. "This is fascinating stuff, Sir George. If this is true, Darwin's theory of evolution has just gone out the window. This answer is just incredible. The answer on the dinosaurs is just as fascinating.

"Well, Sir George, thank you for being honest in your conclusions. I would like to keep this letter if you don't mind."

"Certainly, ma'am."

"I expect you're getting tired, Sir George. I won't keep you any longer. If I can help in any way to finalize what's going on, please ask."

Sir George was just about to reply when the phone rang. The prime minister lifted the phone, and George saw her pale visibly. She put the phone down.

"I'm afraid I've some bad news, George." The prime minister's exclusion of "Sir" meant it was serious in Sir George's eyes. She continued, "Your house has just been blown up, George. If you will sit there, I'll find out more and get back to you."

The prime minister rose and left Sir George. He sat there feeling numb; he only hoped Gorvik was alright.

The prime minister came back in about fifteen minutes. Sir George was in control of himself as she entered.

"I'm sorry, George; I'm afraid it's the worst. Your house was blown up with what the Special Branch estimated was a thousand pounds of explosives. There were no survivors; Gorvik and your two security men were killed outright."

Sir George's control had evaporated. The prime minister went over to him and laid her hands on his shoulders. "You can stay here, George, till we find out who's responsible for this atrocity."

Sir George looked up. "Thank you, ma'am, but I've still got my London flat to go to. If it's alright with you, I'd like to leave now, ma'am."

"Certainly, Sir George, but first I'll arrange for someone to go with you." Sir George didn't protest at this. He knew that she had contacted Special Branch and would have him watched for security reasons.

Half an hour later Sir George was on his way to his London flat. The prime minister said before he left that she wanted him back at Downing Street with McAlister at or before three-thirty. She said she was sorry to have to bring him back, but it was too important not to. The driver let Sir George out at his flat off Grosvenor Square. He would collect his own car when he returned to Downing Street.

I was sleeping soundly when the phone rang. I glanced at the clock; it was four in the morning.

"Hello," I said.

"It's me, David—Sir George."

"Yes, Sir George?"

"I'm afraid I've got some more bad news for you, David." He then told me what had happened at the house while he was with the prime minister.

I was wide awake on hearing the news. "Do we know who did it, sir?"

"No, David, we don't."

I asked how the meeting with the prime minister went.

Sir George replied, "Do you think this is the time to discuss that, David?"

"No, sir. My mind is just getting used to what happened to Janet."

"Okay, David, we can talk some other time. You will have to keep me informed about what's going on from now on, as Gorvik's dead."

I hadn't had time to think of that. "Did Gorvik tell you anything about today, sir?"

"Yes, he told me about his premier being assassinated at four o'clock today. I've informed the prime minister."

"I'll call you tomorrow sometime, Sir George, and we can talk some more." With that I hung up. I lay back on the bed. I couldn't shed any more tears for what had happened to Gorvik; I had shed them all for Janet. I felt more alone than at any time in my life. I was filled with thoughts of revenge for Janet and Gorvik.

I had to put this from my mind. Tomorrow I had to go to America and see if I could convince them of my conviction that what was going to happen in the future was true and only days away from being final. In six days' time the world as we knew it would cease to exist. The prediction for yesterday had come true, and I fully expected the one for today to happen as well. I got up from bed and went to my jacket on the chair. From the inside pocket I pulled out the rest of the predictions. I sat on the bed and read them over. This was the twentieth time I had read them over, so I knew them by heart, but they were so revealing in what they contained it made me shiver every time I read them. The prediction for Friday was going to be important to the U.S.A.

The prediction was about North and South Korea. On Friday, the eleventh of June, hostilities would break out between North and South Korea at twelve noon. I knew this would involve America, as they were committed to helping if this should happen. What I had to think about was when to tell the Americans. They would think I was just another nut, or they might contact my government for verification of my sanity and what they thought of what I had told them. Sir George and my prime minister may tell them of past predictions that had come true and that my prediction could be true this time as well. If this happened, the Americans might move early, before the prediction time had been reached.

I made up my mind to tell the Americans one half hour before the actual event took place. This would leave them very little time to do much about the prediction. I would have to explain the reason why the prediction had to be fulfilled as predicted, so that the powers that be realise the truth of the last prediction.

It was Friday. I had been woken by another phone call from Sir George. We had talked of the death of Gorvik and the two security men. Sir George had told me that the media as a whole thought the attack on his house had been done by the IRA; this was put out to throw anyone off getting hold of what really happened. Gorvik had not been mentioned in the casualty figures, as the Home Office had no way of explaining who or what he was. I agreed this was the best course. In the back of my mind were thoughts of why the disciples hadn't helped Gorvik to survive the blast or used some miracle of theirs to make him better. This planted a small seed of doubt in my head, but it was gone as quickly. There was no time left for doubt, only action. I told Sir George what was going to take place later today. Sir George spoke of Thursday's prediction and the reaction from his colleagues. "And the prime minister has told me to tell you, David, she wished you every success in the conclusion of your task, and the cabinet is now wholly behind you, David." This was the best news I had heard for days. Sir George then asked for a repeat of today's prediction and time. I told him North and South Korea would begin hostilities against each other at 11:30 P.M. that night. Sir George groaned and then I told him not to tell the prime minister until the eleventh hour had been reached. Sir George agreed.

I had thought the two agents sent by the president would

have let me know the day they would leave, but no word had reached me on why the delay. I wanted today's prediction to be passed to the president by me personally. I wondered what route the Americans would take to America. If they went by normal charter, they might be too late to tell the president the prediction.

EIGHT

Chester Manns arrived back at the American embassy and entered by a side door to which only a few of the embassy staff had a key. He headed for Harry Black's office right away. On entering the corridor he saw Joe Simms leaving Harry's office. Chess hesitated until Simms had disappeared through another door, then entered Harry's office quickly, sweating profusely. Harry was sitting behind his pinewood desk. He glanced up, then sat up bolt upright. The colouring and state of Chester told him something was very wrong.

Harry spoke first. "Where the hell were you, Chess? I've been trying to phone the safe house but getting no reply. Did Martin get to you? He and one of his buddies had me hogtied for a little while. I didn't talk even though they did this." Harry held up his bandaged hand. He hadn't thought of phoning Chess until much later, as his hand had been giving him too much pain. He was still looking at Chess and telling him how he had escaped, and including the lie of not having talked.

With his story done, Chess told him to shut up and listen and flopped down on the chair facing Harry. "The girl's dead, Harry."

"So what, Chess? That's what you were supposed to do when you got the information from her."

"That's what we planned, Harry, but it all went wrong."

"You mean Martin got to you?"

"No, Harry, just listen. I told Simms to leave. I didn't want that wimp around when things got hot with the girl. I had her tied up and was questioning her when she managed to free

92

herself. She struggled with me and I accidentally stabbed her with a pair of scissors."

Harry sat for some seconds then stood up. "So you accidentally stabbed her when she got free," he said.

"Yes," Chess replied.

"You're a liar, Chester. Simms told me what state the girl was in when he left, and struggling with you, never mind escaping, didn't seem possible."

"It's the truth!" Chess shouted.

"Then you won't mind me bringing Joe Simms in to hear your story."

"No!" Chess cried. "No need for that." He told Harry the full story, the truth this time.

When he had finished, Harry said, "I thought Martin got you as well. They knew where you and the girl were hiding out; they let it slip when they questioned me."

Chess was too dazed to pick out Harry's lie.

"So you thought you would enjoy yourself before getting any information." Harry smirked.

"I want out, Harry, and I want out now; get me stateside as soon as possible."

"How the hell can I get you stateside? What do I tell Foster you went home for?"

"I don't care what you tell him, Harry; just do it."

"I'll see what I can do, Chess. Now tell me, the girl's body, have you got rid of it?"

"No, it's still there as far as I know."

"I'll get the cleanup squad to make it look like murder." Harry lifted the phone and called a special number. These people were not connected to the embassy, nor were they ever in contact with it, although they were agents. Harry gave the information over the phone with instructions to make it look like a vicious murder by someone unknown. The cleanup squad would take the body from the house and dump it with various false clues as to why Janet was murdered, which would throw the police onto a false trail.

"Well, that's that taken care of, Chester. Why don't you go and clean yourself up? It will make you feel better."

"Nothing will make me feel better, Harry; just do what I asked and get me home."

As Chess got up to go to the door, it opened and in walked Joe Simms. "Sorry, sir, I didn't know you had anyone . . ." He never finished what he was about to say. When he recognized who the visitor was Manns's state told him something had gone wrong.

Chess brushed past him without a word and went out the door. Joe looked at Harry and asked what happened. Harry told him the girl had been in an accident and was killed.

"You mean that bastard killed her?"

"That's right, Simms. Chess killed her. She was a traitor and working for another country."

"Bullshit, sir." Joe turned and left.

There was a knock on my hotel-room door. I took the gun from my jacket pocket and opened the door slightly. It was the two agents. I let them into the room.

"Where the hell have you two been? You were supposed to have taken me to America yesterday."

It was Fred Bloom who answered, "We're sorry, Mr. Martin, but certain events overtook our immediate priorities. Your girlfriend Janet, for one."

My chest tightened at the mention of her name. "Do you know who killed Janet?"

"Yes, Mr. Martin. It was Chester Manns, on Harry Black's orders."

"How do you know it was him?"

"Joe Simms told us after the story was published that she was murdered by people unknown and found in an alleyway."

94

I made a promise to myself to avenge Janet's death when this was all over.

Fred Bloom interrupted my thoughts of revenge. "We leave for America in a half hour, Mr. Martin. We should leave right now if we are to catch our flight."

I asked how long it would take to get there and our arrival time.

"We're going by Concorde, Mr. Martin, and should arrive at the White House about seven o'clock this evening."

I gave a sigh of relief. I would have plenty of time to tell my story and relate the coming event, which would involve America in the Korean conflict. I asked both agents what they drank and called down their order. The Americans ordered scotch on the rocks, and they seemed to enjoyed them. The three of us left twenty minutes later. I was just glad to be on the move again.

As we stepped out the hotel's main door, Eddie Sinclair went to get the car from the hotel car park. Fred and I heard the shots at the same time. We both looked at each other, then ran round the corner of the hotel to where the car was situated. We were in time to see Eddie return some shots at a Ford Escort trying to leave the grounds. The Escort's front window shattered and the car ploughed into the other two stationary cars. Fred Bloom and I ran over to the Ford Escort. The front window had completely shattered on impact with the other two cars. We looked in. It was Chester Manns. He was dead. The bullet had taken him just above his left eye; the back of his head was nonexistent.

Eddie came over. There was a dark stain growing on his right shoulder.

"What happened?" Fred asked him.

"I just got the car door opened when that bastard started popping off at me. I got hit in the shoulder; the rest you saw for yourself."

"How did he know where to find us?" I asked.

"Beats the hell out of me," Eddie said.

I looked at Fred. He just shrugged his shoulders.

"We better get out of here, Fred," Eddie said. The three of us got into the car Eddie had gone for. There was a bullet hole on the side of the door. We drove for the airport.

Eddie's shoulder wasn't as bad as we thought. It had just been grazed. He put a clean handkerchief on it. I suggested we stop at the first chemist and buy a decent bandage. Harry heard the news about Chester Manns on the afternoon news. He and Chester had had a talk with Joe Simms and Joe blurted out his conversation with the other two agents. He tried to stop himself, but Chess threatened to kill him then and there. The way Chester had put it to Joe didn't give him much choice. "You've ratted me to those two bums," he had said to Simms, "so killing you don't make any odds to me. I can't go stateside now because of you, so tell what you know, or I'll kill you right now."

Joe told what he knew; then Harry told him to wait outside the office till he spoke to Chester.

"Look, Chester, take that idiot with you and get the three of them as they come out of the hotel."

"That young bastard's on their side, Harry; he'll never agree to killing them."

"Tell them if he doesn't agree, you'll kill him."

A smile appeared on Chess's face. "Okay, Harry, we better go right now; we only have an hour before they leave."

Chess left Harry's office and grabbed Joe's arm in the corridor. "Listen, son, you're coming with me." Chess half pushed, half dragged Joe out of the embassy.

When they got into the red Escort Chess told Joe what they were going to do. Joe said, "No way, Chester, you're on your own with this one."

He made to get out of car when Chess pulled the gun

from his pocket. "You'll do as you're told, sonny, or I'll blow your head off."

Joe closed the door again and just sat there. Chess started the car and drove off the embassy grounds. He was sure the kid would try to escape if the opportunity arose or try to stop him if he could. Chess drove out of London as if he was going to the airport to stop Martin and the two agents. Joe's hopes rose; it would be nearly impossible for Chess to do anything at the airport, as it was very security-minded.

When Chess took a turn away from the road leading to the airport Joe didn't notice. It was a quiet country lane where Chess stopped the car. "I forgot to take a leak at the embassy," he said to Joe, "and I don't trust you to sit here while I do it, so get out and stand over the other side of that fence where I can see you."

Joe got out and climbed the fence. He looked at Chess.

"Feel safer now?" Joe said.

"Sure do, kid." At that Chess pulled his gun out and shot Joe in the guts. Joe doubled over onto the wire fence, still alive. Chess grabbed his hair and pulled his face up. "I'm going to put you out of your misery, sonny," and with that shoved Joe backwards onto the grassy field. As Joe went backwards Chess shot him in the head.

Chess was laughing and talking to himself as he got into the car. "Now for those other three bastards," he said out loud. He turned back towards London and his original plan of killing them at the hotel car park. Chess's mind had cracked; his eyes were staring and a grin of sheer madness showed on his face. "Now for you, Martin, you bastard," he said out loud as he raced back to London.

The agents and I arrived at the airport in plenty of time for our flight. I had taken the decision to phone Sir George and John, to tell them where I was going. Sir George didn't seem surprised when I told him whom I was going to see.

Sir George said he thought it would be the Americans after I had told him about the Korean prediction. He hoped I was successful in whatever way I handled the situation. He then asked if I had any more information I wished to convey to him. I replied that I hadn't and that I would see him when I arrived back. When I called John he wanted to know everything. I told him I didn't have the time and had just called to tell him where I was heading and whom I was meeting. John's reaction was a loud whistle over the phone. When he had calmed down he wished me luck. Fred Bloom came to the phone box and signalled that it was time to go. I told John I would see him in a day or two and hung up.

The two agents and I boarded the Concorde without further incident. We took off on time. I let out a sigh of relief as the plane left. I ordered a drink and contemplated my meeting with the president, but my thoughts returned to Janet. At least the bastard who had killed her was dead as well, but this thought didn't seem to ease the pain I felt for Janet. I shook these thoughts from my mind and realised that it was only ten days ago that my friends and I had been enjoying ourselves at the embassy party. Eddie Sinclair interrupted my thoughts by asking what the president wanted to see me for. Fred Bloom looked at Eddie as if that question shouldn't have been asked. I told them both that it was a story they might not want to hear or believe when I did tell them.

I decided to relate part of the story and omit anything that would jeopardize my meeting with the president. After they were told the story, they both asked if I really believed it myself. At this I just shrugged my shoulders as if maybe I didn't believe it myself, but I was tired of talking and just closed my eyes. They didn't question me anymore and let me sleep; what

I had told them would give them plenty to think about till our arrival.

I woke with a start. Fred Bloom had nudged me awake. "You were talking in your sleep, David."

"Was I? Did I say anything you could understand?"

"No, just the name of that girl who was murdered."

I changed the subject and asked how long we had to go before landing.

"One hour," Fred replied.

I had slept for three hours.

I ordered myself another drink. I sipped it for ten minutes, then went to the toilet to freshen myself up for my meeting with the president. When I returned I must have looked apprehensive about meeting him, for Fred told me not to look so worried, that the president was an okay guy. This made me smile. I could just picture Fred looking at the president in that frame of mind.

We landed at Dulles Airport at six-twenty. I was feeling more confident when we were ushered through customs without any delay. Fred and Eddie showed some passes, which must have been of the diplomatic type, as no hold-up was evident.

We came out of the main terminal building. The sun was still bright in the sky, and it was very humid. Eddie pointed to a black limousine parked about thirty yards down from the main exit building. As we approached, the front door opened. The man who got out looked of Latin origin, maybe Italian. He smiled as we approached. I was about one yard behind Fred and Eddie and they were about ten yards from the car when the other door opened. Another man got out, only he wasn't smiling; he had a submachine gun in his hands. Fred was first to see the danger. Eddie was just seconds behind, but they were both too late. Fred shouted for me to run. I didn't have to be told twice. The machine gun started firing. I didn't stop to look around.

I managed to reach the main terminal car park and dived behind the first parked car before looking across to where Fred and Eddie were. They were about thirty yards from where I was. Eddie was on his knees. I could see his shirt front was saturated with his own blood. He was trying to level his gun on his assailants, but another short burst from the parked car threw him on his back; it was obvious that he was dead. Fred was lying facedown in the other direction. He had taken the full force of the first volley, and it had spun him round; he was also dead. The gunman didn't seem to be in too much of a hurry to escape until some more people came out of the terminal building and women started to scream at the blood that covered Eddie.

The back door of the limousine opened, and I could see the face and one arm of whoever it was shouting to the gunman to get into the car, which he did with great speed. The face at the rear of the car looked towards where I had run. He couldn't see me of course, but that didn't stop me from ducking down and waiting till I was sure they had left. I stooped down until I was farther into the car park, which was immense. No one from the terminal building had seen me run over here; neither did any of the stationary taxi cabs parked some hundred yards farther up the main terminal.

I stood up and looked about me; the urge to panic came and went just as fast. *What the hell do I do now?* I thought. The airport police were on the scene of the shooting, and I could hear police sirens in the distance. I had about fifty pounds on me. The idea of changing it before leaving England hadn't occurred to me; there hadn't been any time to do so anyway. The thought occurred to me that the airport bank would change my money to dollars, but the risk of the killers having someone in the terminal was too great. I had to make a decision soon before the killers sent another car back to look for me.

I had decided to chance one of the taxicabs to take me to the nearest bank. The first one I asked didn't mind taking my British pounds for where I wanted to go, but all the banks were closed he said. I had forgotten about the time.

"Look," I said. "How much to drop me off near the White House?"

"In your pounds, buddy? Twenty of them."

I looked at him for some seconds, then asked if he would take some of my English money and change it for dollars.

"How much are we talking about?" he replied.

"Counting the fare, fifty pounds," I said.

"Okay, buddy, I'll give you twenty dollars and take you where you want to go. How's that?"

"Great," I said. All the time I wanted to smack him in the mouth. I knew I was being stung badly, but beggars can't be choosers. "Let's go," I said.

On the way he gave me twenty dollars and I handed him my fifty English pounds. He dropped me at the Lincoln Monument. As I got out he shouted, "You be alright, buddy?"

"Sure," I said in my own impersonation of his American accent. He drove off a happy man, I thought. Strangely enough, I had never been to America and knew very little of what twenty dollars would get me. I had formed a plan of action in the cab while the driver had blubbered on about nothing I could remember. First I had to get to a telephone kiosk and try to contact Sir George or John. Trying to get into the White House by myself would be useless. Sir George would have to phone his many contacts and get them to pick me up at a prearranged spot.

I found a phone box, but it had been vandalized; that made me feel as if I were back in Britain. I eventually got to one that worked.

I was confused at first but managed to work out the number for assistance. I dialed the operator and she answered right away. "What number please?" she said.

"Look, I'm a tourist and would like to call London. Could you tell me how much it will cost?"

"Direct to London will cost you thirteen dollars for five minutes, sir."

I let out a "bloody hell," then apologized.

"That's alright, sir," she replied.

"I'll call back, miss," I said. The phone went dead.

I only had eight dollars in change; the rest was paper money. I looked at my watch—ten to eight. Time was passing and I only had till eleven to see the president before the prediction came true.

There didn't seem to be any shops nearby that would give me the change I needed. Then it dawned on me. "Fool," I said to myself, "why not reverse the charges?" I called the operator again and told her the number I wanted. She asked if she could call me back if it was accepted. I gave her the necessary details of who was calling and to whom I wanted to speak. I put the phone down and waited what seemed like hours, fretting in case someone else wanted to use the phone.

The time elapsed was only six minutes when the phone rang. I grabbed it quickly and heard Sir George's reassuring voice ask, "Is that you, David?"

"Yes, Sir George," I replied.

"Are you alright, David?"

"Yes, but I can't make a move without someone taking me in to the White House."

I was about to explain when Sir George interrupted me by telling me what had happened. He had been telexed half an hour after the incident had occurred. Sir George explained that he had got in touch with our people here before I had left and if there was any trouble he was to be contacted.

"We knew of the shooting, David, but you weren't mentioned so we assumed you had got away and we alerted our embassy in Washington in case you tried to contact us there."

I thanked Sir George for his foresight and asked what he could do to help me now.

"Give me your location, David, and someone from our embassy will pick you up and take you in to see the president."

I gave Sir George my location and waited for someone from the embassy to pick me up. Twenty minutes later a car drove up to the phone booth. I was standing across the road, not trusting anyone. The small flags on the bonnet of the car convinced me that it was ours; they showed the Union Jack.

When I got to the embassy car it was an old friend from the Foreign Office who greeted me. "Hello, David," James Donovan said. We shook hands. "We hear you've had a rough time of it lately."

"That's an understatement, James," I replied.

"We've been told not to ask anything about what you're doing here, David, just convey you to the White House when you're ready to go."

I looked at my watch again—eight-fifty-five. "Do we have time for me to get a change of clothes at our embassy and for me to see the president before eleven, James?"

"Yes, David. The White House is only a mile from our embassy."

"Thanks," I said and relaxed in the comfort of the car.

In our embassy I was introduced to our ambassador in Washington then rushed to a room where I showered and put on a borrowed suit that fit me better than my own one had. It was nine-fifty when we sat down for some late dinner before I left to see the president. There were three others at the table—the ambassador's wife, James, and the ambassador himself.

The ambassador said, the same as James had said in the

car, "We wish you luck, Mr. Martin. We don't know what your mission is about, but it must be of national importance if it involves the president."

I nodded my head in agreement with what he had said. It was ten-thirty and time to leave. I thanked the ambassador and his wife for their hospitality and left with James.

Five minutes later we were entering the White House gates. Security men checked out the car and occupants. We were then shown into a private room to await the president. James was still with me and said he would be waiting outside for when I was finished with the president. I kept glancing at my watch—ten-thirty. I was beginning to get nervous again; then the door opened. The president walked in with a man James introduced as Mr. Foster, the president's security adviser. We all shook hands and the president said, "Sit down, Mr. Martin." As we sat down, James excused himself and left.

I looked at Mr. Foster again; something was very familiar about him, as if I had seen or met him before. I put Mr. Foster to the back of my mind and started to tell the president why I wanted to see him. Before I got into the story in depth I requested that Mr. Foster should leave, as what I had to say was for the president alone. Mr. Foster jumped up in protest, saying that he was trusted completely by the president and should stay. The president overruled him and told him if this was what Mr. Martin wanted, so be it. Foster stormed out of the room. That's when I realized I had seen him before—he was the third man in the car at the airport.

I wanted to tell the president about it right away, but this wasn't the time to distract his attention with something else.

"Mr. President, do you have any knowledge why or how I am here?" I asked him.

"Your prime minister has tried to put me in the picture, but I'm afraid most of it was over my head or, to put it bluntly, Mr. Martin, very unbelievable."

104

"I understand that, Mr. President. It was some time before I was totally convinced myself. I will tell you the whole of the events that have taken place up to now."

After I had reached the incident at the airport the president said he was sorry about that and his people were looking into it but without much success.

"Well, Mr. President, I know you have been patient in listening to this story and there are questions you wish to ask, but at this present time I cannot go into them in detail, as what I have to tell you next will, I hope, convince you of the truth of what I have told you." I looked at my watch—eleven-ten. "In twenty minutes, Mr. President, North and South Korea will be at war with each other."

He sat down astounded at this comment. "Is this one of those predictions you were telling me about, Mr. Martin?"

"Yes, sir."

"But if this is true what is the point of telling me at this point in time?"

"This prediction is just one of many which have taken place and will take place over the next five days. You are being informed in this manner so that you and other world leaders who are involved in this can prevent the final prediction coming true."

"What is the final prediction, Mr. Martin?"

"The final prediction, Mr. President, will be a total nuclear war between the United States and the Soviet Union, with no survivors anywhere in the world."

"How is this to happen, Mr. Martin?"

"I'm afraid I can't relate that information until you and the others are convinced that it will happen so that all of you will take the correct action to stop it. The information that is required to do this will be given to you on the fifteenth of this month. This will, we hope, give you the foresight to avert this

105

final prediction from coming true." I glanced at my watch again—eleven-forty.

Just as I did so the door opened with a rush. "Mr. President, you had better come quickly. North and South Korea have gone into open conflict."

I looked at the president. His face was ashen; he sat staring at me as if I would tell him how to stop it. He rose very slowly to his feet and said, "Thank you for what you have told me so far, Mr. Martin. I am not so much certain of the truth of what you have told me; I'm more afraid." At this he shook my hand and said he hoped to hear from me. I said he would and thanked him for his time.

As I watched him leave, the change in his appearance from when he came into the room was very noticeable; he was a very worried man.

"I'll show you the way out, Mr. Martin," the man who had told the president the Koreans had gone to war said.

"Thank you," I replied and followed him to the waiting embassy car.

James was already inside. He asked if I heard about the Koreans.

"Yes," I replied sadly.

James was excited by the prospect of being busy back at the embassy because of the outbreak of war between the Koreas. I didn't feel like talking about it; I just let James ramble on.

Back at the embassy it was busy, as James had said it would be. I had one more thing to do before I left on a morning flight. I got hold of the ambassador, with James in attendance.

"I would like you to tell the president that his top adviser is the same man who tried to kill me at the airport."

The ambassador asked, "What adviser?"

"The one in intelligence, a Mr. Foster. His first name is

James. I saw him at the White House when the president came into the room."

"I'll take care of that, David; you go and get some sleep."

I *was* feeling strained and tired. I thanked the both of them and left for my room. My flight home was at nine on Saturday morning.

I woke at seven and was given bacon and eggs for breakfast. I had then read the American papers, which were full of the war and two hundred American dead on the border with North Korea. I put the papers down when James appeared.

"Are you ready to go, David?"

"Yes," I replied.

The ambassador came out of his study and said, "I hope you have a quieter journey home than you did coming, David."

I smiled, shook his hand, and left for the airport. The journey home was uneventful. When I got off at the London airport, Sir George and three other men were there to meet me. One I knew was John; the other two I hadn't seen before.

Sir George embraced me like a long lost son, which was out of character for him, but I accepted it with grace.

John was smiling and grabbed my hand and shook it firmly. "Glad you're home, David," Sir George said. "These other two men are from the department; not ours, I might add." They were security men from MI6 which was obvious by their quick glances around looking for would-be assassins. The five of us got into what looked to me like a funeral hearse but was obviously some imported foreign saloon car. The windows were dark so you could look out but no one could see in.

While we drove to our destination, Sir George explained it was in the country. "The reason," he went on, "is that you are now being sought by various people who want to find out how you can tell the future."

I knew what Sir George meant in his roundabout way; there must be still some agents from whatever country still trying as they had been from the start to get information and kill me. I accepted Sir George's information without argument. He went on to tell me that he and John would be staying with me for as long as it took to settle this thing, as Sir George called it. I nodded my head in agreement. There was nothing I could do but give the predictions right before they happened and pass them on to Sir George at the correct time. He would then give them to the right people so that the final one could be averted.

The place we arrived at was not unlike the one Sir George had—a sprawling mansion with a great many trees surrounding it.

"Well, what do you think, David?" Sir George asked.

"It's great, Sir George, just great," I replied. I didn't want to tell him a bed-sit would have done me, as that would have hurt his ego.

John said, "It's got everything, David, swimming pool, games room, and even a tennis court at the back. I'll give you a game if we've got time, David." John seemed to be enjoying this assignment. I told him he would be too easy for me, and he laughed and asked, "How much?"

The inside of the place was as good as I knew it would be, as Sir George had picked it. A couple of paintings here and there looked to be done by the old masters. The ceiling had been done by excellent craftsmen in gold tints with murals interlaced. The carpets were like walking in soft sand; your feet sank into them.

Two elderly people came out of what I took to be the cook's quarters. Sir George introduced them as Jeannie and Sam. "They will be looking after us all for the duration of our stay here." Jeannie said that tea would be served in ten minutes. The man called Sam asked if we would like a stronger drink, to which Sir George replied, "Maybe later, Sam. Thank you." After further investigation of the house we selected our rooms. I told Sir George I would speak to him after I washed and changed. My clothes had been brought from my flat, which I hadn't seen for about two weeks.

When I was ready I knocked on Sir George's door. He was standing at the mirror with the electric shaver when he called me to come in. "Yes, David, what do you want to talk to me about?"

Again I looked at my watch—six-twenty. Time seemed to be the only thing I could concentrate on, as it was the most important part of my role if the predictions were to be believed. "It's another prediction Sir George."

He switched the razor off and gave me his full attention.

"At six-forty, Sir George, Spain shall make an attempt to take back Gibraltar."

"Do you mean by force, David?"

"Yes," I replied.

"Bloody hell, David, couldn't you tell me earlier?" He then said quickly, "I'm sorry, David; I forgot you have to tell me at the time specified."

He didn't finish his shave but went quickly to the phone, which was what I wanted him to do, as my telling him and no one else knowing wouldn't help anybody. I left the room and went to find John. I knocked on his door, and he replied that he would be down in ten minutes. As I sat there my thoughts wandered to Janet. If only she were still alive this would seem much easier to do. Knowing that people were going to die and you couldn't do anything to help until it was too late was beginning to tell on me, but I also knew that many more would be saved if the plan worked.

John came dancing down the stairs. "Where's my Ginger Rogers?" he shouted.

I called back, "Will Jeannie do?"

He shouted again, "In a house like this anyone will do!" As he got nearer he said, "Let's get drunk, David."

I said, "That's a great idea, John. Let's see what Sir George thinks."

He was also coming down the stairs. He heard the both of us and said, "I think it's a great idea, lads."

I couldn't picture why Sir George agreed. The prime minister wouldn't be happy and was likely to let Sir George know it.

The two security men didn't get in on the binge that the three of us started. It was two in the morning before the last of us succumbed to getting to bed. Sam had to help all three to make it up the stairs. For once Sir George showed that he had been drinking. His staggering from one side of the banister to the other, even with Sam's help, gave that away. John had passed out at one o'clock. I had tried to give Sam some help with him but only managed to make things worse by falling over the fireplace rug. Sam managed John by himself. I was last to go up and felt proud that I had outlasted the both of them.

Sam agreed with my gibberish of how well I had outlasted them. There was a smile on his face as he let go at my room door.

"Good night, sir."

"Good night, Sam."

The last I remember was turning the door handle and shooting across the floor towards the big bed. I didn't think I'd make it.

I woke up with the biggest head I'd ever had in my life; it throbbed. I hadn't made the bed last night. I was still half in, half out of it and fully clothed. Even with the pain in my head I laughed. If I was in this state, the picture of Sir George and John's condition wasn't worth thinking about.

We met at the breakfast table about half past nine. John

110

looked like a disaster, but Sir George looked his immaculate self, which sort of disappointed me. Jeannie laid out the breakfast, which was scrambled eggs and toast. John turned two different colours of green and asked to be excused as he rushed towards the nearest toilet. Sir George asked how I felt. I lied. "Just great, Sir George." He smiled. Jeannie dropped a spoon on the table that hit a saucer. Sir George's hand went to his temple. He saw that I noticed and withdrew it quickly. We both looked at each other and went into fits of laughter. Even Jeannie joined in. We had just got it under control when John appeared and started us off again.

We sat and had nothing stronger than tea after breakfast. I mentioned to John that if he had any more bright ideas to keep them to himself.

"God," he replied, "how did I get to bed?"

"Sam took you up," I said.

John blushed slightly, and we started laughing again. John asked me in a more serious tone how long I thought we would stay here.

I looked at both of them and decided to tell them the final day of reckoning was just three days away. "We should be over the worst by the sixteenth of this month," I said.

Sir George tried to get some more information from me about the other predictions, but I refused to offer any. I told Sir George that the next prediction was only a matter of hours away. It was one o'clock that the next event would take place, and it was only eleven o'clock now. I asked John if he felt like playing a game of tennis to sweat the drink from our bodies. He said, "No, but I'll play."

We were still on the tennis court when I called Sir George over for the next prediction. It was one hour before the event happened. Sir George looked apprehensive.

"Don't look so worried, Sir George. This one isn't so bad to take, but I want the president of the United States to be informed right away after you tell the prime minister. Mount Etna will erupt again for the last time. It will nearly halve itself with this eruption."

"Very good, David," Sir George said with obvious relief.

John and I finished our game. He owed me a fiver.

"I'll get a shower and try you at snooker, John."

"You're on, David."

John and I were playing snooker when we next saw Sir George. He came up to the table and said that he had some interesting news from America. "It seems," he said, "that a certain official in the White House has had a fatal road accident." Sir George didn't have to tell me who; it was Foster. John asked who he was. I told him that Foster was part of the same group of people who had killed Janet. Sir George listened to the radio for any news on Mount Etna. True to the prediction, it erupted at one o'clock, as the newscaster announced. "At least any people who were in the vicinity of Mount Etna had been saved by hours' warning beforehand," Sir George commented.

The phone rang before Sir George said anything more. Sam lifted the phone as we watched. "It's for you, Sir George," Sam said.

Sir George took the call, he didn't say much to whoever was calling, just an occasional "yes." He turned to both me and John and said, "That was Tom McAlister. He thought we would like to know that an agent from the American embassy has just been dragged from the river Thames; his name is Harry Black."

John was the only one to speak. He said, "The Americans are cleaning up their own house in double quick time since you saw the president, David."

I just nodded in agreement with him.

The next two days passed quickly. I had given Sir George another two predictions. One concerned Cuba and the death of Fidel Castro. That was on the fourteenth. On the fifteenth, which was today, I told him what was to happen. This time he was very agitated at the content of the prediction. I told him one of the royal family would die today at two o'clock. As it was one-forty-five already, he couldn't do anything but tell the prime minister what was to occur. He asked if I knew who was to be killed in this accident. I replied that this information wasn't available to me.

All our nerves were too tense to really be upset too much with that particular prediction. Tomorrow was the final day of the predictions, and Sir George and everyone else involved would be on tenterhooks until I told them the final one, which was to be the most important one, and everyone knew this. Sir George had told me the president and prime minister had both contacted the Russians and kept them informed of all events predicted. What the Russians finally believed would be known tomorrow.

It was seven o'clock on the sixteenth of June. I had given Sir George the last prediction early. At twelve o'clock last night I had told him that Israel would drop a nuclear bomb on Damascus at four o'clock on the afternoon of the sixteenth. Sir George was shocked, to say the least. He asked me why this should happen if the predictions were to try and stop it in the first place. I told Sir George that the prediction was given so that this would be the only nuclear bomb used. The Americans and Russians would have to be convinced of the total destruction of the planet unless they joined forces to stop the escalation when the Israelis dropped the bomb.

I told Sir George that the prediction mustn't be given until the prime minister and others involved would not take any action until the prediction had happened. Sir George had protested that they couldn't stand by and watch all those people die when we could maybe prevent it. The prime

113

minister had spoken to me on the phone with the same kind of protest. I explained that any change in prediction either by interference from us or any other superpower could prove more disastrous than the prediction. She agreed after some deliberation with advisers of her cabinet.

At 3 P.M. the three of us were pacing up and down the parlour of the mansion, each with a drink in his hand. Sir George had said that if we were still alive at five o'clock the worst would be over. Four o'clock came and went; the news had come in that Israel had indeed dropped a bomb on Damascus. At five o'clock more news came, that America and Russia had taken steps to try to stop the war between the Arabs and Israel.

Sir George jumped up from where we had been sitting on hearing this. "Let's get stoned, you two. We've done it." He corrected himself, "Well, we did help, David."

We shook each other's hands and did get stoned, as Sir George had put it.

Just before we got drunk the prime minister called to tell us how pleased she was and that the American president sent his regards to David Martin. I was back at my own flat twenty-four hours later. The three of us had been told to take a week's break from our duties. Sir George had surprised us all by telling the prime minister that he wanted to step down from his post as foreign secretary and retire from politics. I had also told Sir George that I was giving up my junior post. John was more upset at this announcement than Sir George or anyone else. But he saw why I would be happier, as there were too many bad memories. I didn't mention Janet, but she was never out of my thoughts.

We spent some time with the prime minister, who handed me a telegram from the American president thanking me for my efforts in stopping a potential nuclear war. The Russians also sent a note of thanks. They would never admit that the predictions were the cause of their cooperation, but I told the prime minister to thank them anyway. There were two agents put outside my flat to keep an eye on me. The prime minister said they were only there for added protection until this had finally died down.

They had all asked if the people who had told me the predictions would be in touch with me again. I lied that they would not be in touch again; she would never take the agents away if I told her the truth.

It was two days later that Peter finally came. I was sitting in my flat watching television but not really concentrating on it when Peter appeared.

"Well, David, you have succeeded in your task and my master wishes to speak to you."

I looked about me as if Jesus would appear at any moment.

"No, not there, David," Peter said. "We shall go to the place where it all started."

I knew before Peter told me where that was—the old farmhouse on Holmoor Road.

"There's two of my country's agents stationed across the road, there for my protection. They may follow me."

We walked past the two agents, and they didn't blink an eye as if we didn't exist. I took my own car and on the way I was tempted to ask Peter why they allowed Janet and Gorvik to die. I was very nervous, more nervous than at any other time in my life, including all that had happened to me recently. When we arrived at the farm Peter got out and told me that he would be leaving me. I was just about to protest to Peter while looking at the farmhouse when I turned round to find Peter had gone.

It was then I noticed how peaceful the surrounding countryside was, no noise, not even a bird calling. I looked along the Holmoor Road, not even a car in sight. I went up the path to the door, which was slightly ajar. I went in after taking a deep breath. There he was sitting behind a small table. His garb was like Peter's; his hair was down to his shoulders just as my image of Jesus had.

He spoke first.

"Sit down, David."

I did so meekly. As I sat down I looked at him more closely. His eyes, like Peter's, shone as if a bright light was inside them. The feeling of peace was also not so much seen but felt.

He started to speak to me again. "I am very pleased with you, David. You have suffered much in carrying out your given task. You have lost some friends and loved ones. For this I can only say for you not to let it prey on your mind, as all will be revealed to you in time."

I wanted to ask the same question that I was going to ask Peter, but refrained from doing so. He then asked me if I wanted to ask him anything other than about the task I had carried out. I stammered before getting my thoughts together. I had thought a lot about certain things I would ask if this meeting ever took place, but now I was here I couldn't bring myself to ask them; it would sound too much like I doubted who he was.

He spoke as if he had read my very thoughts. "I will give you some answers to questions which many people have," he said. "If I am Jesus Christ, the Son of God, why do I allow small children to die of starvation and wars to take place and people suffer all types of pain? Well, David, all the wrongs of your world are created by man himself. Millions die of starvation while others, because of profit margins, have mountains of food, enough to feed all the starving millions. This therefore cannot be laid at my Father's door. Wars are started by man's greed for more wealth; instead of cooperating with others, he kills them and achieves nothing. I could go on, David, but you will see that most of man's troubles are created by himself."

I then got up enough courage to ask him a question myself. It came out faster than I meant it to. "Is there a life for us all after death?" I blurted out.

"No, not for all, David. As has been written, David, my Father's door is open wide, but the road to it is very narrow. Most arrive at my Father's door and most enter, but there are those who break his teaching and shall never enter his house." He went on, "Those who have everything and give little to those who need something will find my Father's door closed, for what could my Father give them that they do not have, except eternal life, which they do not deserve?

"Does what I say lay your doubts at rest, David?"

I replied in a timid voice that I never doubted him.

To this he said, "I will tell you what to do next, David. Now that you have given up your chosen profession, I want you to write a book about this episode of your life."

I sat there stunned. "But I thought this was not to be known to all people," I replied.

He said, "I myself will be returning to the people in fifteen years; this will be known as the Second Coming. Before my return half the people who inhabit this earth will perish, as has been written."

I was amazed at this statement and asked how the people would die.

"They shall die of a disease not yet known to man but created by him. This disease shall take every second person who lives," he said.

I was about to ask him about his Second Coming, as he called it, when he said that time was coming to a close for this meeting. "Before I leave you, David, I want you to put this little question in the book which you will write: What two people are different from all the other people, alive or dead? This includes me, David."

I sat there wondering what two people were different from all the rest of us.

"It would take you some time to work it out, David, so I will tell you who they are. Adam and Eve," he said. "They do not have bellybuttons." He was laughing at this time, and I joined in his laughter.

When the laughter had stopped he stood up and said that it was time to go. He thanked me and told me to write the book as quickly as I could. I stood and watched him go out the door; the feeling of being at peace with myself was still with me after he left. When I left the farmhouse the noise of the countryside was back and cars were passing by at the bottom of the farm.

During the time I was writing the book the prime minister retired from politics and the president of America died. Most of the people who were involved in the predictions either died or retired from their places of power.

I stayed in the house for nearly a year writing my book. John came round now and again, but this also got less frequent. It was one year to the day after all this began that I finished my book. During that time my thoughts always strayed to Janet and what might have been. I took my book to a publisher, and he told me he would publish it. As I stepped out of the publisher's I didn't feel very happy at having written a book and gotten it published. I should have been elated, but there was just this feeling of emptiness. There was a small downpour as I waited to cross the road to my car; then someone called my name as I stepped off the curb.

I looked round. It was my old workmate John. The next thing I knew, Janet, Peter, and Gorvik were coming to meet me surrounded by bright light. I looked down as Janet came to me. Down below there was a crowd, including John, leaning over someone who had been hit by a bus after stepping off the curb.